"I don't even know you..."

"Clearly there's chemistry, but I can't get sidetracked by a sexy man who came to my rescue."

"I obviously wasn't looking to get sidetracked, either, but there's nothing I want more than to lay you out in front of that fire and give you exactly what your body is aching for."

There should be some major red flags going up. A stranger coming in at the exact time Stella needed someone, the fact he knew precisely what to say...

Dane brushed Stella's hair from her face, letting his fingertips feather across her jaw before he pulled her mouth to his.

She didn't even try to fight the kiss... Why would she? They'd been building toward this moment since they met.

A kiss from Dane Michaels was powerful, toe-curling, panty-melting and instantly had her mind on sex.

And she was more than ready to take him up on his offer...

* * *

Montana Seduction is the first book in the Two Brothers duet from *USA TODAY* bestselling author Jules Bennett.

Dear Reader,

I'm beyond thrilled to bring you two fun, sexy stories involving twin brothers Dane and Ethan. Up first is Dane, a recluse who just wants to gain back his late mother's property so he can go home to his ranch. Oh, but I have something much more exciting for him than a quick in and out. He won't sneak off that easily.

Stella wants this resort for herself and has no clue her competition is the late owner's son! Oops! This could get tricky, especially since they get along so well behind closed doors.

I'm a sucker for combining a multitude of tropes so I hope you enjoy the close proximity, stranded in a snowstorm, mistaken identity, twin combo in *Montana Seduction*. I'm also all for a strong shero who knows what she wants and gives the hero a good challenge. This was definitely one fun book to write!

I hope you all enjoy Dane and Stella and look forward to the next book featuring Ethan.

Happy reading!

Jules

JULES BENNETT

MONTANA SEDUCTION

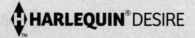

Recycling programs
for this product may
not exist in your area.

ISBN-13: 978-1-335-60382-1

Montana Seduction

Printed in U.S.A.

USA TODAY bestselling author **Jules Bennett** has published over sixty books and never tires of writing happy endings. Writing strong heroines and alpha heroes is Jules's favorite way to spend her workdays. Jules hosts weekly contests on her Facebook fan page and loves chatting with readers on Twitter, Facebook and via email through her website. Stay up-to-date by signing up for her newsletter at julesbennett.com.

Books by Jules Bennett

Harlequin Desire

The Rancher's Heirs

Twin Secrets
Claimed by the Rancher
Taming the Texan
A Texan for Christmas

Texas Cattleman's Club: Houston

Married in Name Only

Two Brothers

Montana Seduction

Visit her Author Profile page at Harlequin.com, or julesbennett.com, for more titles.

You can find Jules Bennett on Facebook, along with other Harlequin Desire authors, at Facebook.com/harlequindesireauthors!

To Lori Foster,
who spoke at the first writer's meeting
I ever attended *a few years ago* and
has turned into a great friend.
Thank you for everything!

One

Getting dumped only days before the wedding and spending the romantic mountain honeymoon at a fantasy adults-only resort by himself was humiliating. What could be worse than going on a honeymoon riding solo?

Or at least, that was the response Dane Michaels was counting on.

Sympathy could be a powerful tool, and he planned to use it in his favor. No one would have the slightest suspicion about the poor, abandoned man staying at Mirage Resort and Spa—and by a combination of laying on the charm and playing on everyone's solicitousness, he should be able to get all the information he needed.

So did it really matter that Dane had never actually had a fiancée—never intended to marry? The lie had embedded itself so deep in his head, he was more than ready to play the part of the jilted groom.

Dane pulled his truck to the front of the resort. The four-story lodge seemed suspended on the side of Gold Valley Mountain and with each guest suite having one-way windows from floor to ceiling, nearly every angle offered a breathtaking view of the valley below.

Gold Valley, Montana, had been his mother's first choice when opening Mirage. She'd had a vision, a life plan. But before she could fulfill her dreams, she'd suffered a fatal stroke, and her bastard husband, Robert Anderson, had taken over the two Mirage resorts and left Dane and his brother, Ethan, penniless and alone.

Dane exited the vehicle before the valet could assist him with the door. Dane wasn't here for the amenities or the secret rooms designed to fulfill couples' fantasies. He was here for one purpose and one purpose only—to find his opening to get this resort back in his name where it belonged, so he could honor his mother's memory.

Slipping the attendant a couple of Benjamins, Dane headed up the stone steps leading to the grand entrance. Nostalgia threatened to suck the breath from his lungs, but he pushed on, determined to get exactly what he came here for.

He hadn't been back in so long for several reasons. Mainly because he didn't want to return until he was sure he could secure this place for himself. The time had come.

Ignoring the pain of being back nearly two decades after his mother's death, Dane steeled himself against any emotions. He hadn't gotten this far by being soft and sensitive. Dane had been smacked with a dose of reality at the age of eighteen and life had been a giant kick in the ass since.

Everything he'd done, he'd crawled and fought for until he got back the money, the power due to him… there was just one thing left.

Without a glance to any of the couples milling about in the open lobby, Dane headed straight to the front desk to check in, reminding himself to remain constantly aware of those around him. There was no room for error and no time to waste.

Dane had a nearly twenty-year-old promise to fulfill.

Mirage manager Stella Garcia had no clue who he was, had no idea her world was about to change. Mustering up charm and sex appeal wasn't exactly Dane's area of expertise anymore, he left that to his playboy brother. But right now, and for the foreseeable future, Dane would use every other tool in his arsenal to pull those family secrets from this stranger to get back what belonged to him.

Once upon a time, a seduction would have been

Dane's method of choice for an operation like this. Back then, he didn't have to try to get a woman into bed, they were more than willing to follow.

Fighting overseas in Iraq had changed him, hardened him, made him even more hell-bent on getting what he deserved.

It had also left him scarred and horrendous.

Getting close to anyone, let alone being sexual, had been practically impossible ever since. He wasn't stupid or naive. He knew what he looked like, knew doctors said there was hope if he wanted to go through painful surgeries in an attempt to cover the scars.

He didn't need to cover them. They went far beneath the surface of his skin so some vain attempt at erasing the past was a moot point.

And that had been the sole reason as to why he'd been reluctant to follow through on this plan. But when he couldn't think of another way to get what he wanted, Dane realized this might be the only way to gain full control of Mirage.

Besides, he needed a distraction from his own mind, the prison he'd been trapped in since coming home from Iraq. He'd thought getting his hands dirty and working from dusk till dawn at his ranch would exorcise the demons away, but they were still waiting every single night.

From the photos he'd seen of Stella, flirting with and charming her certainly wouldn't be a hardship.

"Charming" wasn't his default mode, but he could turn it on if he needed to. And presenting himself as an abandoned groom seemed tailor-made to winning her sympathies and softening her reserve.

He sure as hell hoped his act of vulnerability and loneliness got her to trust him, to open up and give him a glimpse of exactly how he could use her to get to her father. Presenting himself as some woman's reject chafed at his pride, but he'd put up with it so he could gain the information he needed. Then he'd head back to his ranch, make this deal a legal thing and no one would even care about his initial plan.

Of course he'd have to hire someone to run the resort. That person would have to be trustworthy and loyal. Dane would accept nothing less than the best for his mother's place.

Dane kept his sunglasses firmly in place and quickly checked in, turning down the offer to have his bags taken to his room. He knew the way. There was nothing about this resort he didn't know. A few things may have changed—the decor, the staff—but the layout hadn't. He'd practically grown up here.

Dane had booked the largest luxury penthouse, the one he knew matched the owner's penthouse. They were the only two suites with a mini pool and oversize hot tub off the enclosed bedroom balcony. Lovers could literally take just a few steps from their bed and sink into the pool or hot tub while overlooking the beauty of the mountains and valleys.

All of the rooms were top-notch, but Dane wanted the best. After all, wouldn't any groom plan the most romantic getaway and spare no expense?

As he stepped into the elevator, Dane removed his glasses and pocketed them. Once he put his things away, he had every intention of going out and "accidentally" running into Stella. He knew her schedule, knew every single thing about her thanks to the investigator he'd hired. Dane's knowledge of her schedule and her personality were the keys to gaining her trust.

Dane was well aware that her father treated her like shit and that he'd given her only six months to prove to him that she could run this place and show a profit—a mammoth undertaking after years of mismanagement had nearly run Mirage into bankruptcy.

Getting Mirage for himself was the main goal, but besting the arrogant bastard who treated his daughter like some bothersome employee was going to be icing on the proverbial cake. Victory was always sweet but victory over assholes was just plain fun. Dane was willing to admit he wasn't exactly an angel himself, but at least he was a smart and careful devil.

Dane left his bag in his suite, taking only a moment to admire the open view and spacious room. The wall of windows made it seem like he was suspended above Gold Valley. The curved pool was just as inviting as he recalled.

Later he would fully take in the beauty of the

room his mother had designed. The stone fireplace, the balcony, the high beams stretching across the ceiling.

For now, though, memories would have to wait. He had a woman to find.

"What do you mean he didn't show up?"

Stella Garcia attempted to tamp down the migraine that threatened to further sour her already stressful, overloaded day. She stared at one of the hostesses for their main dining area and Stella thought for sure the poor girl was going to burst into tears.

Tears solved nothing—a life lesson Stella had learned from the start. Her mother had died after complications giving birth, ultimately leaving Stella with the most unloving father.

For reasons Stella still tried to wrap her mind around, she wanted his approval—craved it even. Would do anything to earn it, even if that meant taking on impossible tasks.

Which was how she found herself in the current situation—running a top-tier resort with a crowd of hungry patrons about to descend for dinner…and no cook.

Maybe if she'd had her mother, maybe if she'd had just one parent who pretended to actually care…

"He called and said he quit, effective immediately," the hostess said, nervously tucking her short blond hair behind her ear. "He said something about moving back home to his wife in Oregon."

Stella pulled in a deep breath and wished she could fast-forward to midnight when she could go up to her suite, pop open the prosecco and unwind.

Unfortunately, at this rate, she didn't even know if she'd get to bed tonight. All-nighters were depressingly common with this job. Some days were certainly more difficult than others, but she had to keep reminding herself that she'd inherited a mess from the previous manager and her father thought her incapable of fixing it. Those were two highly motivational reasons to prove to the whole damn world that she could and would make Mirage the greatest, most talked about resort on the globe.

"Our guests will start rolling in within an hour," she stated, tapping her finger on her chin as she thought out loud. "I'll need to see if there's anything already prepped or if we have to start from scratch. I know zilch about cooking."

But she could make a spreadsheet on the financial analytics of nearly any type of business and never break a sweat. She actually loved business and numbers. Damn, she was such a nerd. Too bad her hobbies hadn't included donning an apron and sizzling steaks.

Her young hostess shook her head. "I burn Pop-Tarts, so don't look at me."

If Stella had the time, she'd call up her now ex-chef and verbally shred him. But using her energy to get angry wouldn't solve their problem. For now, she simply had to push that employee out of her mind because at this point, he was irrelevant.

Really, it was better that he was gone. She didn't want anyone working for her who wasn't loyal. There was no room for mistrust or laziness, especially when she was on the verge of getting Mirage back on its feet and finally taking charge of her own life.

"Maybe Martha could help," the girl suggested.

Stella shook her head. "No, she's off because her sister is getting married. Damn it. She would've been able to salvage this evening. She's an amazing chef. I don't even think Raul is coming in until Friday. I may have to call him in because we are in a bind. But I doubt he'd get here in time."

Employees' names raced through her mind. It was hard to think of any options. The kitchen staff had the perfect rhythm down and worked like clock-work...well, they did until someone decided to up and quit. But the synchronicity meant no one really stood out as someone who could be trusted to take over the kitchen, even just for one night.

"Okay," Stella stated as she tucked a wayward strand of hair behind her ear. "We can do this. There's a logical solution, I just have to figure it out."

"Excuse me?"

Stella jerked her attention to the double wooden doors leading to the bar and private seating area.

She was about to say they weren't open yet, but her words died in her throat.

Hello, cowboy.

That charcoal-and-red-plaid shirt tucked into well-worn jeans did nothing to hide the beautifully muscled bulk of the mystery man in the doorway. Those shoulders stretched the material of his shirt and his silver belt buckle shone with some emblem she couldn't quite make out.

Well, she could if she wanted to get caught staring at his junk, which wouldn't really be the classiest move. Not to mention it would be totally unprofessional of her since he was a guest…and likely here with his significant other.

Shame, that. This man might be worth the risk of forgetting her duties and obligations, but she preferred her men to be available…unlike the jerk who thought she was his ticket into the family money— and that she was too dumb to uncover that he actually had a girlfriend with a kid on the way.

Yeah, no thanks, asshole.

Stella pulled her mind from the nauseating memory and opted to focus on the living fantasy standing in the doorway.

But that man would just have to stay a fantasy— along with every other man for the time being— because anything or anyone taking up her time would mean failing at her job, and her father was just waiting for one little slipup to sell this place out from under her. Her sole focus had to be on Mirage.

Smoothing down her button-up shirt-style dress, Stella took a step toward the striking man with dark eyes. "Our dining room doesn't open for another hour. Did you need to make a reservation?"

Which he totally should, because there was plenty of divine food prepared by an experienced chef. Part of Stella wanted to laugh at the snarky comment inside her head, because she'd realized over the past few months that if she didn't laugh, she'd have a nervous breakdown.

But at this moment, she worried that her laughter might border on manic or deranged. She was so, so close to getting what she wanted. There was no way she'd let a rogue chef thwart her plans.

"I couldn't help but overhear that you're in a bind."

That whiskey-soaked voice had her shivering and the vivid fantasy she'd tried to push to the back of her mind kept rushing to the front. Wasn't there some resort rule about lusting after a guest? After all, this was an adults-only resort so he probably wasn't here alone. A man who looked like that likely never slept alone…while she knew no other way.

Oh, she wasn't innocent, but she never stayed the night in someone's bed, and over the past year she'd barely dragged herself into hers. She'd been working her ass off for her father, wanting to gain his approval, wanting…hell, something from him other than disdain.

Getting Mirage running like a dream was her last chance at some type of parental nod.

"I might be able to help," the stranger added.

Stella crossed her arms and smiled. "Oh, well, that's not necessary, but thank you."

"Do you have someone else to cook?" he asked.

Oh, that dark arched brow that accompanied the question had her belly quivering with unwanted arousal. She must be sexually deprived if a brow and a voice turned her on. Well, the whole rough, manly-man exterior also gave a healthy punch of lust.

Maybe she should examine that belt buckle a little closer.

"Are you a chef, Mr…?"

"Michaels. Dane Michaels." In two strides he was in front of her and offering a half grin that drew her eyes down from his perfect teeth to the dark stubble covering his jawline. "I'm not a professional chef, but I'm a damn good cook. Ask any employee on my ranch."

His ranch. Of course someone this rugged and mysterious had a ranch. Montana had no shortage of cowboys, but this guy…he was the real deal and no doubt hands-on with his work if those weathered lines on his face were any indication. Likely the emblem on his buckle was that of his ranch.

"Mr. Michaels—"

"Dane," he corrected and had her toes curling in her boots with that full-fledged smile. "And you are?"

"Stella Garcia. I'm the manager of Mirage." Soon to be owner…she hoped. "Dane, I can't ask a guest to come into the kitchen where food is being prepared."

He propped his hands on his narrow hips and held her gaze. "You didn't ask and I don't see that you have many other options right now. Do you?"

Well, no, but that didn't mean this was a good idea. She couldn't let a stranger just come in and ride to her rescue. Good heavens, if her father heard of that, she'd definitely be reprimanded.

"Stella."

She turned to the Mia, the hostess Stella had completely forgotten was even in the room. "Yes?"

"We just got three more reservations and that booked us up for the night. That doesn't include the fantasy rooms and the room service." Mia chewed on her lip and stared over Stella's shoulder to the fantasy man. "I mean, you should at least think about his offer, but do it fast because in forty-five minutes, people will start coming in."

Stella rubbed her head and tried to remind herself that she wanted this job, that she loved Mirage. So far she'd had one headache after another, but for the most part she'd been cleaning up the mess left by the previous manager. Apparently he'd been a jerk to the employees and now Stella was paying the price of the resulting disloyalty. Loyal employees didn't leave without giving notice.

But she did want to own Mirage. True, she wanted her father to see her as a valuable businesswoman and a capable daughter…they were all the family each other had. But more so, she wanted this place because she'd heard of the woman who built it. A single mother who branched out to create something spectacular all on her own.

How could Stella not admire that and strive to be as strong as the original owner, Lara Anderson? When her father had acquired the resort, Stella had done her research on the place before her father let her in this position. She did that with each of his acquisitions, but this one had always stuck out to her and she'd had her sights set on it for years.

"I can't believe I'm considering this," Stella muttered as she spun back around to Dane.

Had he just been checking out her ass?

Well, well, well.

No. That should not excite her. She'd been in a relationship several years ago with a guy whose eyes, and other body parts, wandered a bit too much.

Stella cleared her throat. "I couldn't pull you away from your significant other."

"I'm actually here alone," he countered.

"Alone?"

"It's a long story," he added with another slight

grin—this one looked a little pained. "I'll tell you about it while we prepare dinner. Deal?"

Stella shouldn't go along with this. The idea of letting a stranger, a *guest*, into the kitchen was preposterous, but at this point, she wasn't sure what other option she had. She needed help and she'd be in there the entire time watching to make sure nothing lawsuit-worthy happened, so what could go wrong?

The worst choice would be to do nothing and stand here and have a mental debate with herself. If her father happened to find out what she'd done, she'd be more than happy to defend herself and be proud that she'd pulled this ill-fated night out of despair…so long as this stranger could do all he'd promised.

Stella nodded toward the kitchen. "Follow me, Mr. Michaels."

"Dane, remember?"

As she led the way through the dining room, she felt very aware of the intriguing stranger following closely at her back. She worked with men every single day. Her father was one of the most powerful men in business and had a slew of minions in suits that worked for and with him. None had her in a fluster like this one.

There was certainly something to be said about a mysterious, attractive man riding to the rescue at the eleventh hour. It was like fate had planted him right in her path.

And the fact he was here alone had her even more intrigued. Stella couldn't imagine there wasn't a line of women with lingerie packed and ready for a getaway to a fantasy resort with this guy.

"There should be several starters made up in advance," Stella began as she pushed on the swinging kitchen door. "Let's hope that's the case tonight."

"Either way, it will all work out," he told her.

When that velvety voice washed over her, she wanted to believe him, but considering they were coming from two different positions, she wasn't sure she should be so quick to let her guard down.

"The menu is set up two weeks in advance so we can have enough supplies ordered in—that means we have a direction on where to go." Stella pointed toward the wooden board hanging outside the walk-in refrigerator. "I know we'll have everything for tonight's menu, it's just putting it all together like it should be that's the challenge. And well, I'm not known for my kitchen skills."

Dane stepped around her and placed a hand on her forearm. That warm, rough palm slid over her skin and had her wondering just how those hands would feel over other, more neglected parts of her body.

Now was not the time for her dormant hormones to come rushing back to the surface.

"I promised it would all work out, right?" he asked. Those dark eyes held her in place. "Trust me."

"That's a bit difficult since I don't know you," she

stated as she stared into those midnight eyes framed with heavy black lashes. "But for now, I'm going to have to trust my instincts and roll with this plan."

His thumb stroked over her arm. "I'll make sure this all works out. For both of us."

Suddenly, Stella wondered if he wasn't just referring to dinner.

Two

Dane had originally thought his plan was going to be easy, but getting in the door had taken charm and a little flirting. He was usually so good at getting information he needed.

Both actions painfully outside of his comfort zone these days, but he'd taken a page from his younger, more social brother, Ethan.

For now, Dane would act like he was the most confident, suave man Stella had ever seen. There would be no cause for her to be suspicious. Soon, she'd trust him with all sorts of secrets, and after that, the resort would be his in no time. Finally, after all of these years.

And all he had to do was get close to a striking, sexy woman. Cooking was going to be the easy part, and hopefully this instant foot in the door would give him that extra boost he needed when it came to capturing her trust and attention.

She'd certainly captured *his* attention with no trouble at all.

That first glimpse of Stella when she'd turned around had nearly rendered him speechless. Thankfully, he'd remembered why he was here and that any distraction, no matter how sexy, could cost him everything.

Just because he was here to get close to her, didn't mean he could lose sight of the prize.

But then the rest of the kitchen staff started milling in and Stella went to work and took charge. While Dane figured out what the hell he needed to do to create a dinner for one hundred–plus people coming in and out over the next few hours, he also managed to watch Stella in action, knowing that would give him insight as to how to handle his next steps with her.

Damn if she wasn't even sexier when she focused on her own goal. He knew she wanted this resort for herself, he also knew her father wouldn't let that happen. The old bastard was stringing her along and had no intention of giving his daughter anything.

While Dane had never met the man in person, watching him from a distance and hiring an investigator to dig up details had shown that Ruiz Garcia was the biggest male chauvinist jerk Dane had ever heard of.

But that was just one more weapon in his arsenal—a point of connection between them he could use to create sympathy and trust. They both had bastard father/stepfathers and they'd both lost their mothers.

Once all was said and done, and he'd secured Mirage, Stella would see that he'd actually done her a favor by getting her out from under the thumb of her controlling father.

Until then, well, Dane would have to do a little more socializing than he'd planned. The pleasure of spending time with a sultry, alluring woman would make up for the comfort zone he'd stepped so far from. She was responding to him nicely so far—he just had to make sure that he kept up the act...and that he didn't let her expose the ugly, scarred parts of him, whether they were visible or not.

There was one obstacle after another, but that end result...

Several hours and countless dishes of pork roast with mashed potatoes later, Dane worked on the cleanup. The rest of the staff had been dismissed and Stella was out in the dining room straightening everything.

Dane certainly wasn't a star chef, but being raised by a single mother had given him an edge in household tasks. Lara Anderson had been adamant that her boys do every bit of work deemed for "women" and she swore she'd make them good husband material. His mother wasn't here to see that neither of her sons had any intention of being a husband, but Dane was still thankful he'd paid attention when she'd shared her special recipes and guided him through basic preparation steps.

Most of the dishes were washed and put away. From the checklist, it looked like all Dane needed to do was prepare a few things for the breakfast crowd. The fruit needed to be cut and placed into separate bowls. The bread was all ready to go, it just had to be put out at room temperature.

The more Dane did, the more he missed his ranch. Being alone and feeding just one was more his speed. His cattle could fend mostly for themselves and the horses were like his best friends. Aside from his ranch hands, those animals were about the extent of anyone or anything he wanted to care for.

Soon, though. Soon he'd be out of here, with the property in his name and then he could figure out how much time to spend at the ranch and how much to spend here. The penthouse he'd gotten for this stay would be a perfect suite for him to keep, but he knew the owner's suite was even more spectacular. His mother had spared no expense when she had brought her dream to life.

"Well, you saved my ass."

He'd admired said ass quite a bit since first step-
ping through the dining room. The sway of her little dress as the hem hit the back of her knees. Those
tiny buttons that ran down the middle of the front
had teased him all night. He'd stared at the one just
between her breasts as if willing it to slide right open.

Dane wondered what she wore beneath and opted
to use his own imagination. He figured Stella to be a
lace type of lady. Someone like her would want to be
all business on the exterior yet all woman beneath.

His body responded instantly to the image of her
with the dress stripped away, her dark hair around
her shoulders and her breasts bound by lace.

Dane slid the sharp knife through the juicy strawberry, but didn't glance up at Stella. She came to
stand on the other side of the stainless prep area and
rested her palms on the flat surface. If Ethan were
in his place he would've cleared off this island and
had her beneath him in seconds.

Dane wasn't Ethan. Revealing his body by taking
Stella to bed wouldn't seal the deal—it would sour it,
once she saw what he was hiding under his clothes.
No, there wouldn't be sex—just flirting. Teasing.
Winning her trust slowly and carefully. Well, as
slowly as his sanity would allow. He wanted Mirage in his name right now, but he knew he had to
be patient.

"Happy I could help," he finally replied, attempting to get control over his hormones. He needed to

pace himself. "I'm just going to get this fruit cut up and set in the fridge. What time should I be here tomorrow?"

"Oh, no," Stella retorted. "You've more than helped. I called in our part-time chef and offered an exorbitant amount of money if she would cover for the next few weeks."

Dane stopped slicing and set the knife down as he lifted his gaze to hers. "That wasn't necessary. I would've helped while I was here."

Stella smiled. Not the flirty smile he often got from women when he ventured out, but the type of smile that contained a sense of…pity.

Damn it. He'd seen enough of that from his staff at the ranch when he'd get lost in his war nightmares. He'd let the majority of them go because he did not need sympathy and he didn't want anyone in his house hearing his cries. He refused to take pity from anybody and he sure as hell couldn't afford to have it from the woman he was trying to get close to.

But pity from Stella was a bit easier to handle. She didn't even know the real reason to pity him, so technically her emotions toward him right now were null.

"It's not like I had anything else to do," he replied. "Besides, it wasn't bad and I got to help a beautiful woman."

Stella pursed her lips, but she didn't even blush. He'd have to reconsider his verbiage. Clearly she was either used to compliments or she wasn't interested in them. Either way, he had to tread carefully and keep working to build a connection between them.

"I'm sure you could've done just fine on your own," he amended. "I can't imagine you would've let a rogue chef ruin the night."

Stella crossed her arms over her chest and cocked her head. "I don't let anyone ruin my plans once I set them into motion."

Perhaps they had even more in common than he'd initially thought. Which would make this entire process that much easier…once they got over this initial get-to-know-you phase.

"That attitude is why this place is so successful." He flashed her a smile and picked up a strawberry, extending it across the island toward her. "You're an admirable woman."

She kept her eyes on his as she took the fruit from his hand. "I've already comped your room for the duration of your stay. Flattery isn't necessary."

Comped his room? Wasn't that adorable. He had enough money to buy this entire resort and not put a dent in his finances, but the fact she'd done so just proved she was sincere in her commitment to Mirage…and her father didn't deserve such loyalty.

"That wasn't necessary," he replied.

With a shrug, she bit into the strawberry. The second her lips closed around her fingers to clean away the juices, Dane was pretty damn thankful he had a barrier between his waist and her eyes.

Was she purposely taunting him? She'd been so all-business before, he'd thought he'd have to be the one to initiate all the flirting. Only one of them could take the lead and he'd already signed up for that position. No way was he going to be sidetracked.

On the other hand, if he'd already gotten her curiosity piqued, his work here could be over sooner than he'd planned.

"I believe you owe me a story," she told him after she finished licking each finger and driving him out of his mind with want. He wanted that mouth on him. "We got so busy you didn't get a chance to tell me how someone like you is at an adult resort all alone."

At least this part he'd rehearsed and prepared for. He didn't know how to hide his actual arousal because that sure as hell wasn't an act and not planned...at least not standing in the resort kitchen.

"I'm on my honeymoon."

Stella stared at him a moment before she let out a sharp laugh. "And you left your wife at home?"

"Actually, my fiancée opted to leave me a couple days before the wedding."

Her smile vanished as her brows shot up. "You're serious."

Dane nodded, pushing forward with the lie that rolled easily off his tongue. "Humiliating as this is to admit, yes. Apparently ranch life wasn't for her and she decided to reconnect with her ex. I thought about canceling the reservations, but I figured I deserved a getaway so here I am. I hope that's not against any house rules."

Stella pulled in a deep breath and made her way around the prep island. Dane shifted to face her as she came to stand before him.

"Not at all. We don't usually get singles, but there's no rule." Stella's dark eyes held him, captivated him. "Your fiancée is either a moron or undeserving. You're better off without her."

"You don't even know me. Perhaps she's the smart one."

Stella reached over and plucked a cut berry from the chopping board and held it out to him. "I realize we just met, but I'm a good judge of character. I'd say you're pretty noble and loyal."

Loyal? Hell yes, he was loyal—to a very select few. There were only two people in this world he'd do anything for: his twin brother, even though their personalities were completely opposite and they rarely saw each other, and his mother.

His mother was the sole reason for this charade and his brother…well, they each had their own thing going in trying to track down the bastard who stole everything from them once their mother passed. Yes, he knew plenty about loyalty. But he was about as far from noble as he could get.

His plan to take her father down and reclaim what belonged to him might be devious; it might be cruel, even. He wasn't proud of that. For all his faults, he'd never been selfish, he'd never purposely been deceitful. But he was about to do a hell of a job now because the future of his mother's legacy was on the line. With honor on one side and loyalty on the other, his choice was clear. There were no rules for him.

"Looking back, we could best be described more as friends than anything," he added. He didn't want to come off as a complete prick for flirting with Stella right after ending an engagement. "I'd gotten used to the idea of not being alone and being a couple was more habit than anything. She found someone and they're in love. She's happier now."

"And you?" Her question came out in a slight whisper. "Are you happier now?"

Dane swallowed the strawberry and licked his lips. Her eyes darted to his mouth and he wondered if seduction really could be this easy. No wonder Ethan always had a new woman. Still, this wasn't Dane's typical behavior. There was no going back now, though.

Not with the chemistry crackling between them even though he hadn't even laid a finger on her. Damn…he wanted to get her into bed. Even though it wasn't in the plan—even though it might ruin everything—the temptation was growing stronger with every passing moment. Something shifted, something he couldn't quite place a finger on.

Lust. He hadn't expected this strong of a pull. He hadn't wanted a woman in so long. Well, he had natural urges, but to actually feel the desire and the ache…he couldn't recall the last time. Granted, avoiding people in general probably contributed to his lack of sex life. But sex or getting close to anyone would open the door to questions he wasn't ready to answer.

In the last several hours, Dane found he actually wanted to get closer to Stella. That could be the lack of sex in his life talking, though.

"I'm happy that the marriage didn't happen," he stated. "When I marry, I plan for it to be a one-time thing."

He nearly laughed at that statement because he rarely left his ranch, let alone dated anyone. Dodging people and any social activity had been his new normal since leaving the army, deepening the seclusion that had started with the untimely death of his mother, when he'd opted to keep to himself instead of talk to anyone—even Ethan.

So, no. Marrying was certainly off the table because he'd never let anyone get that close to him. Besides the fear of abandonment again, he wouldn't subject anyone to his nightmares.

"So you do want marriage?" she asked.

"Maybe. Eventually. I'm not in a hurry."

He leaned his hip against the edge of the stainless steel and reached out to push her long inky hair over her slender shoulder. There was no reason for him to try to avoid touching her.

He also needed to get away from this topic because the last thing he wanted her to believe was that he was ready for some fictitious happily-ever-after. The attraction clearly had a place here and that's what he'd hone in on. Any sort of romance had to be left behind.

"You're staying for a week." She smiled and every nerve ending sizzled at that tiny dimple nestled against the corner of her mouth. "Consider every upgrade and meal on the house."

"I can't do that." He shook his head and laughed. "You've already settled the bill for my room. That's more than enough for just helping out over a few hours, though no thanks were necessary."

"Thanks was very necessary," she countered. "Considering I'm riding a thin line and I have someone waiting for me to fail… Well, that's a story for another time."

"So there will be another time?" he asked, not pressuring her on the topic of her father.

Her eyes held his and her smile remained. "As much as I'd like to, I work what seems like thirty hours a day."

"All the more reason to take a break."

"Breaks could cost me everything," she murmured as she glanced away. Then she adjusted her shoulders and returned her focus to him. "It's late and I'm sure you'd like to get to your room and relax."

Only if she came with him.

"I'd relax more if I had some bourbon. Pappy Van Winkle would do the trick, but that's not an option right now," he half joked. "What do you do to relax, Stella?"

Her lids fluttered just a second when he said her name. Good. He wanted her thrown off. He wanted her to be flustered and aroused, thrown off guard enough to let things slip.

"I don't even know what relaxing is," she stated, but he knew she wasn't joking.

"Have a glass of wine with me."

Stella raised a brow. "And what about breakfast prep?"

"I'll finish up afterward," he told her. "I've seen the list and once I get this in the fridge, the rest has to be done in the morning."

"I can't leave a stranger in my kitchen."

Fair enough. "Then help me and we'll get out of here and have that wine."

When she started to shake her head, Dane reached out and gripped her chin with his thumb and forefinger, pulling her gaze directly to his. Those dark eyes held so much emotion. He wondered if she even knew that the pain and the worry inside them was projected to anyone who looked closely.

Had anyone ever looked? Was there someone who took the time to care how much she ran herself ragged? Sure as hell not her father...and Dane wasn't volunteering for that position, either. But she deserved someone. People like Stella worked hard and had great aspirations, but they could get run over.

"Breaks can cost me everything, too," he told her, needing her to know they really weren't all that different, also silently warning himself that he needed to tread lightly for his own sanity. "But I'm willing to take the chance. Are you?"

Three

What was she doing here? Stella had more pressing things to do than to stare at the seam of the closed private elevator doors leading to Dane Michaels's penthouse suite...with a chilled bottle of prosecco in hand, no less.

Maybe she should've brought a nice cab instead? Or bourbon. Hadn't he mentioned a bourbon earlier?

"This is the most ridiculous thing I've ever done," she muttered.

What was she thinking? Just because one mysterious, sexy rancher sauntered in to rescue her, she got all excited and aroused and suddenly couldn't control her desires.

She didn't have time for desires or sexy attractions. Yet here she was heading straight toward both.

The faux wooden doors slid open with a soft whoosh. Stella immediately took in the fitted tee stretching across broad shoulders and well-worn jeans over narrow hips. Dane's hair was wet, making it seem even darker than before. He'd shed the plaid shirt and, mercy's sake, this rancher certainly did the whole hands-on thing. That body made it very clear that he didn't just stay in some office writing checks for his employees.

Clearly Dane had freshened up while she still looked like the haggard mess she'd been since this morning. She should've at least changed, but she hadn't even considered removing her dress and knee boots.

She'd been too busy arguing with herself over why she'd let this virtual stranger affect her so. Maybe she'd been smitten by his white knight routine, but she couldn't just dismiss how ridiculously handsome he was, nor could she ignore how her entire body seemed to tingle with a rush of arousal whenever he got close.

There was something rough and rugged about him. When he'd mentioned a ranch…well, toss her a set of chaps and mount up because that was just flat-out hot. Plus, she'd never ridden a cowboy.

Oh, ranchers and cowboys were all throughout Montana, but none had interested her and she spent most of her time with men in suits who only pretended to know the ranching lifestyle. They'd never do anything labor-related that might mess their suits or smudge their manicures.

Dane rested his hip on the back of the leather sofa in the living area and greeted her with a crooked grin. "So you are a risk taker."

Stella merely held out the bottle of wine and shrugged. "What can I say?"

"You can say that you'll stay awhile."

He didn't stand, didn't move toward her. He simply relaxed there like he was giving her total control, yet that leveled, dark gaze told her who really called the shots. Hadn't she come to him? How could he be so powerful, yet not a bit demanding or even making a move?

The way he stared at her...

Like a lion inviting his prey and she was positive she wouldn't mind being feasted on.

Stella stepped into the spacious penthouse suite. The views never got old, and even from the doorway she could see across the room and stare out the wall of windows. Even in the dark, there was a soft glow coming up from the valley and casting mysterious shadows all over the mountainside.

Lara Anderson had seriously thought of everything when she'd built Mirage on the side of the mountain. No expense had been spared and that's what made Mirage such a magical escape.

If all of these guests opted to come here and get away from their daily stresses, why couldn't she do the same…even if for a short time.

The high-beamed ceilings and dark wood floors made the space appear more like a glorified cabin than a room in a resort. The crackling fire called to her. The stunning feature of the fireplace with its stone surround extending to the high ceiling seemed so inviting…so romantic. No, that was the hot guy that seemed romantic. And she'd brought the wine.

This was too easy. Sex was easy. Seduction was easy. Giving in to hormones and not giving a damn about tomorrow or consequences would be so…liberating.

Unfortunately, she didn't have that luxury of a one-night stand. But flirting and unwinding with a sexy stranger was dangerous ground that she couldn't help but want to dance on tonight. Just one time. That wouldn't hurt anything, right?

"I didn't think you wanted to take a risk."

Stella offered Dane a smile. "I'd say this one is harmless."

Though she knew a man like Dane was anything but. Yes, this was taking a huge chance coming to his room, but, well, her father couldn't control every move she made. She didn't have to justify her personal life to him. All she had to do was prove herself worthy of keeping Mirage and having him sign the property over to her at the end of this six-month experiment. She had only three months to go.

"*Harmless* isn't a word people usually use to describe me," he countered, his dark eyes half-hidden behind lowered lids. That husky voice sent shivers racing through her.

Maybe they didn't use *harmless*, but the word that seemed to embody Dane Michaels was definitely potent. She hadn't even tried to rationalize the hows and whys of this man and her instant attraction to him. What would be the point? Nothing would come of this…whatever this was. Besides, this was fun. When was the last time she'd done something simply because she wanted to? Every move she made had a purpose and an end gain.

Dane crossed the space, keeping his gaze locked on hers. The snap of the fire behind her filled the silence and added to the allure of the moment. The mysterious man, the late hour…the sexual tension.

"Why don't you go have a seat," he murmured. "I'll take care of everything."

Everything? As in…

He slid the bottle from her grasp and she suddenly recalled why she was here. Wine. Not orgasms.

Relax, Stella. Don't make a fool of yourself.

One glass of wine and then she needed to go. Because if she stuck around much longer, she may come across as desperate and not the kick-ass, independent woman she'd fought so hard to be.

"What time will you start back to work in the morning?" he asked as he came over with two very generous glasses of wine.

She wasn't much of a drinker, so if she sucked down all of this she'd likely end up draped over the rug in front of the fire before long. And since "drunk Stella" lacked impulse control, she'd probably be posed in some "come and get me" style that would surely embarrass her once the buzz wore off.

"I'll go back down about five."

Dane settled next to her on the leather sofa and glanced to his watch. "That's in five hours. When do you sleep?"

"When I have time."

Which was rarely. If she could go through these next few months on no sleep, she totally would. There simply wasn't enough time in the day. She had to keep all these balls juggled in the air. Dropping even one could prove fatal for her goals.

"Have you always put so much pressure on yourself?" he asked, taking a drink and then putting his glass on the raw-edged table.

"I don't see it as pressure," she retorted. "There are things I want and failing isn't an option."

"You're the manager of a picturesque mountain resort. What other goals could you possibly have?"

Stella stared into her wineglass. "Not everything is as it seems."

Before she revealed too much, she took a sip and

closed her eyes as the fruity flavors burst in her mouth. She couldn't suppress the sigh that escaped her. That was a great bottle she'd grabbed from the wine cellar.

When she lifted her lids, Dane's gaze had dropped to her mouth and…had he shifted closer?

Arousal churned through her and she couldn't even blame the wine considering she'd just taken her first sip. The seclusion at this late hour and the roaring fire might be impacting her, yes, but not the wine.

"Do you want something more than Mirage?" he asked.

Stella set her glass next to his. The intimate image had her biting on her lip for a just a second before shifting her focus back to him.

"Mirage is all I've ever wanted," she explained. "My father bought the resort several years ago and I'd heard the story of the lady who had built this, relentlessly pursuing her dream. A single mom who pushed through and built something so dynamic and spectacular just hit me, you know? I didn't grow up with my mother, but I just felt pulled toward this strong female, even though I'd never met her. I knew I wanted this business to be mine. My father has plenty of companies around the globe, but this is the one I want."

Dane's eyes seemed to grow even darker, his jaw clenched, but he remained silent. She'd started talking and hadn't even considered that he probably wanted a short, quick answer.

"Sorry," she said with a soft laugh. "I didn't mean to ramble."

"Never apologize for going after what you want."

Stella's smile faltered as she swallowed. "And what is it you want, Dane?"

"That's not so difficult to guess."

Oh, he wasn't subtle. And yet, something about the way he didn't quite come out and say it, but let the implication hang heavily in the air packed an even sexier punch.

"And do you think I came here for sex?" she asked.

"I think you came here because you wanted to know what would happen once we were alone."

"We were alone in the kitchen," she reminded him, clasping her hands in her lap to prevent them from trembling—or reaching for him.

"Not like this." He eased forward, never taking his eyes from hers. "You might not want to take risks, but you can't help yourself. The resort, me… You want to know what it's like to fully throw yourself into temptation and ride out the challenge."

How did he peg her so easily when she'd met him only hours ago? And why did her entire body stir with each low, rumbled word that slid through his lips?

Because she wanted those lips on hers, on her

body. The need crashed through her and took hold like nothing she'd ever experienced.

"I try to have a little more control than that—I'm not as reckless as you make me sound." Or at least that's what she tried to tell herself. "And I'd never take a risk with this resort. Mirage is my life."

"You're quite the professional," he agreed. "But you still took a risk by taking it over. Business isn't for the faint of heart."

"You sound like my father," she murmured.

Dane placed his hand on her knee. "Does he also tell you what a stellar job you're doing?"

Stella eyed those tanned, rough fingers against her dark skin. The hem of her dress proved to be no barrier as the tip of his pinky slid beneath the fabric.

"He, um… No. No, he doesn't."

Mercy, how could Dane carry on a normal conversation? Her body was revved up and she was about to start begging. She really shouldn't deprive her body so long from such a basic, necessary need.

Stella reached for her glass and took another sip. "Let's not bring my father into this."

His hand inched a bit higher, then his thumb slid over the bottom button of her dress as if he would pop it open at any moment.

"Agreed. Everyone should stay out of this room except us."

Stella took another sip and set her glass back down. "We're not having sex."

"Not yet."

She couldn't stop her smile. "At all," she clari-fied. "I can't afford to get caught up in anything but work right now."

Dane's eyes crinkled in the corners as he smiled. "Yet here you are."

Well, he had her there. Stella laid her hand over his and for a split second—okay, maybe more—she wanted to slid it on up and show him exactly how he could alleviate her stress. But she held his hand firmly in place on her bare thigh.

"I don't even know you," she stated. "Clearly there's chemistry, but I can't get sidetracked by a sexy man who came to my rescue."

"I obviously wasn't looking to get sidetracked, ei-ther, but there's nothing more I want than to lay you out in front of that fire and give you exactly what your body is aching for."

The man knew all the right words to say. There should be some major red flags going up. A stranger coming in at the exact time she needed someone, the fact he knew precisely what to say and just how much to press without being a jerk…

No matter the flags, she honestly couldn't find a flaw here.

Stella reached for her glass and tipped it back, taking every last drop of her favorite wine. With a soft clink, she set the glass back down and came to her feet. Dane's hand fell away, and he rose, as well.

"I should get to my room and attempt a few hours of sleep."

Dane brushed her hair from her face, letting his fingertips feather across her jaw. Something flashed through his eyes a second before he curled those same fingers around the back of her neck and pulled her mouth to his.

Stella didn't even try to fight the kiss…why would she? They'd been building toward this moment since they met—did it matter that was only a few hours ago?

Besides, a kiss was harmless. Well, most of them were. A kiss from Dane Michaels was powerful, toe curling, panty melting, and instantly had her mind on sex. The way his body lined perfectly with hers, the way his lips coaxed hers apart, eager for more, only had her more than ready to take him up on his offer.

The wine had gotten to her just as she'd thought it might. She swayed against him, reaching up to clutch his bare biceps. Those were rancher arms. No sedentary job could produce muscles so firm, so…magnificent.

Dane eased back and Stella whimpered. Damn alcohol. She'd never whimpered or begged for any man, yet she'd just done the first and was closing in on the second.

"I'll check on you tomorrow," he told her. "If you need me, you know where to find me."

When he released her, Stella had to concentrate on

staying upright. She hadn't had nearly enough time with him. She wanted more of that whiskey-soaked tone, that dark gaze, those lips and hands on her.

Straightening her dress, Stella pulled herself together and crossed the suite to the elevator. Dane came up behind her, practically pressing her against the doors. Stella closed her eyes and inhaled that spicy, masculine scent.

"I'll see you tomorrow."

The whisper in her ear, the warmth of his breath on her skin had her shivering and with the way his chest was pressed to her back, there was no way he missed her body's reaction to him.

Stella risked a glance over her shoulder. "I look forward to it."

And then she fled back to her room where she replayed over and over the entire evening from the moment Dane stepped into the dining room to the moment he sent her entire body up in flames.

So why didn't she just give in and let him douse them?

No. The real question was, how long would she make them both wait?

Four

Dane sipped his morning coffee and relaxed in the Adirondack chair on the expansive enclosed balcony. He'd come out at sunrise to admire the breathtaking view. He'd had a restless night, thanks in part to one seductress who'd plastered her sweet body against his and left him wondering just who was playing whom.

He'd remained in control of the situation last night, but barely. He needed to have a better grasp of just how potent Stella was before their next encounter. Coming into this whole plan, he sure as hell hadn't planned on questioning his damn sanity regarding his hormones.

Stella had certainly surprised him last night by

coming to his suite. He'd written off seeing her again until today after she'd seemed to reject his invitation. Dane wasn't often taken off guard and finding more reasons to admire Stella was not helping his cause.

He didn't want to admire her, he wanted to use her for her insight into her father's sharklike mind when it came to business. Yet each moment he spent with her, he found himself growing more and more captivated.

Dane had already sent an offer to buy Mirage outright that was more than reasonable, but Ruiz Garcia had turned it down without a counter.

There had to be a way…and Dane was using the method he felt would be the most effective. If the guy treated his daughter like a peasant employee, why the hold over this resort? Why not just sell it, take the money, and cut his daughter out of the business entirely? Why string her along?

So many questions, yet none of them really mattered. All Dane cared about was what it would take for Ruiz to sell Mirage. That was the bottom line.

Dane extended his legs and crossed his ankles. He'd give his brother another hour or so before he called. Ethan was not a morning person, pretty much because he was a nighttime partier. His current state likely involved being wrapped around at least one woman.

While Dane worked here in Gold Valley, Ethan was hoping to work his own magic at the second

Mirage resort on Sunset Cove. The island off the coast of California was certainly more Ethan's lifestyle. Dane preferred his secluded ranch, he thrived in being alone where he didn't have to feed a relationship and had nobody depending on him.

The bond between Dane and his younger brother had been strained since the passing of their mother, but they were still brothers and had two goals binding them together: get back the Mirage resorts and take down Robert Anderson. That bastard had stolen too much from them when they'd been helpless, but now Dane and Ethan were powerful and even more so when they put their resources together. There wasn't a place Robert could hide, not anymore.

None of this was about the money. Both Dane and Ethan could buy any resort anywhere in the world. Hell, they could build something even bigger, better, but they deserved what their mother had created.

With the twentieth anniversary of her death approaching, Dane wanted, needed to feel closer to the only woman he'd ever loved.

Tamping down the ache resonating in the void in his heart, Dane came to his feet and rested his arms on the wrought iron railing. Clutching his coffee cup, he overlooked the valley and felt like a damn king. There was nothing more refreshing than mountain air that was so crisp, so raw.

Dane wouldn't have a difficult time coming off the ranch with picturesque views like this to tempt him. He'd worried about who would actually run the place in his absence once he got Mirage in his control, but the worry seemed less potent now that he realized how comfortable he still felt here. He would be a hands-on owner. This was his mother's place, his mother's dream, there was no way he could turn Mirage over to anybody else.

So long as he kept that in the forefront of his mind, Dane knew he could push through his doubts and fears. If anyone could get him to step back out into society on a regular basis, it was his mother. She deserved for him to step up and put his own issues aside and be the man she'd raised.

Dane pushed off the rail and took the last sip of his coffee. As he made his way through the double glass doors, he pulled his cell from the pocket of his jeans.

There was no time to waste. He needed to discuss things with his younger brother. If that meant disrupting his morning slumber and irritating his bedmates, so be it.

Dane set his coffee mug on the large raw-edged wood island between the kitchen and the dining area as he dialed. He waited for Ethan to pick up, but voice mail kicked in and Dane muttered a curse before clearing his throat and leaving a message.

They were closing in on Robert and Dane was chomping at the proverbial bit to serve a healthy dose of vengeance to his stepfather. Dane wanted to know where Ethan stood and what intel he'd uncovered since they spoke last.

Each day that went by was another day closer to the anniversary of their mother's death and another day that bastard was able to live his life as a free man. Those days were coming to an end and a new chapter in the Michaels brothers' story would begin. Maybe regaining their legacy would bring them back together, closer, like they used to be.

Dane pocketed his phone and headed toward the en suite to shower. While waiting to hear from his brother and plan their takedown, Dane had a lady to charm. And judging from her reaction last night, he wasn't too far from accomplishing all of his goals.

The vibration on the nightstand irritated the hell out of Ethan. Couldn't a guy get a good morning's sleep? If that damn thing kept going off, he'd throw it out the open patio door, not caring if it landed in the ocean.

He turned his face into the soft, warm pillow and blinked against the sunlight streaming in. He purposely kept that patio door open so he could hear the ocean crashing to the shore. Security wasn't an issue—unless a thief who could defy gravity decided to scale the high-rise penthouse. Ethan had confidence he was safe.

Besides, he thrived here. The beach, the ocean, the endless water views from his bed. He'd grown up in Montana and the mountains were fine for his brother, but the second Ethan had set foot on a beach, he knew exactly where he belonged. Everything about this atmosphere called to him and he couldn't imagine spending his life in the mountains like Dane.

The cell buzzed again and Ethan rolled over and smacked the damn thing before pulling it toward him. The screen lit up with a few texts from numbers he didn't recognize and a voice mail alert from Dane.

The texts could wait. Even though they were likely from the ladies he'd met last night and Ethan rarely kept a woman waiting—in bed or out—this business with Dane had to take top priority. They both had their own individual goals, but their joint goal had Ethan sitting up in bed, the sheet pooling around his waist as he dialed his brother.

"Did I interrupt anything?"

Dane's answer in lieu of hello had Ethan grunting and glancing to the other side of his king-size bed. The four-legged, furry feline hadn't stirred since crawling over his face to get to her spot in the middle of the night.

Not many people knew about the fur ball that he'd rescued. But damn it he'd seen the poor lethargic thing out in a storm and he simply couldn't leave it there. Ethan had had every intention of finding a new home for it.

Two years later, they were still together.

"I'm sandwiched between two redheads," Ethan

replied, instead of mentioning the real pussy in his bed. "This better be good."

"I'm at Mirage in Gold Valley."

Ethan felt a swell of pride and anticipation, quickly followed by a dose of jealousy and longing. Dane had already pushed through to the next phase of their mission to gain back what belonged to them, but timing was everything and Ethan wasn't quite ready to make his presence known at Mirage in Sunset Cove.

"I've already gotten close with the manager—who also happens to be the owner's daughter—and it's just a matter of time before I can get the angle I need to get this location back in our family."

Our family. They hadn't been a true family since their mother died. When that happened, Dane had closed in on himself, their stepfather had shown his true, greedy self and Ethan...well, he'd turned to anyone who could make him forget, even if that was for just a night.

"You're moving fast." Ethan threw off the sheet and swung his legs over the side of the bed, taking a moment to enjoy the breathtaking view. "And here I thought I was the charming, irresistible brother."

"You're cocky. There's a difference," Dane retorted. "What have you found out about Robert?"

Ethan raked a hand over his bare chest as he came to his feet. "Right now he's comfortable in Hawaii.

We're so damn close. I want to lure him in. I need him at Mirage in Sunset Cove."

"You're confident you can get him there?" Dane asked.

"He's never been able to turn down the idea of making millions." Ethan had formulated a rock-solid plan, but he needed his brother's help. "If he thinks he can get this resort back and flip it again to make money on it twice, he'll break records getting there."

"Don't make a move until you tell me," Dane stated. "I want to be there when you approach him. We're a team on this deal."

Right. A team. Ethan had hinged his entire life on that…or at least the first eighteen years. But losing their mother had torn a hole through both of them, and they just hadn't been able to reach each other across the empty space. They'd stuck together until they'd both finished high school but then, motherless and penniless, they'd both joined the military and gone their separate ways.

They stayed in touch, calling and texting, randomly getting together, but nothing was the same. Ethan couldn't even blame their polar-opposite personalities. When they'd been growing up, they'd simply balanced each other.

While Dane was more studious, Ethan had been a jock. They could put down an extra-large pizza—covered with sausage of course—and one ate all the edges, the other ate the entire middle. Everything they'd done just seemed to jive.

As adults, well, they were more acquaintances than anything. Their main goal of taking back the resorts and annihilating Robert had always kept them bonded...but Ethan wanted more. He wanted his brother back. In the years since they'd split apart, no one had filled that void. He was always surrounded by people, but he was lonely for family.

"I'm hoping to lure him in within the next month," Ethan replied. "I'll keep you posted."

"I'll do the same from my end." Dane cleared his throat. "We're going to make this happen. For Mom."

The void in Ethan's heart throbbed. "For Mom," he repeated.

And for us.

Five

Stella stifled the urge to breath a sigh of relief at how smoothly the morning had gone with the part-time chef. Thankfully she'd agreed to step up full-time and save Stella's ass.

Considering it was only lunchtime on day one of the replacement, Stella wasn't about to pull out the confetti and celebrate just yet. But she did feel some of the weight ease from her shoulders.

Granted she should be relaxed after that wine and those kisses last night from a virtual stranger, but that sexual tension…

She'd had friends in college who had had one-night stands and Stella had never understood how someone could tumble into bed with a person they'd just met.

Well, now she knew exactly why they didn't let their inhibitions get in the way. Just the memory of that intimate moment had her body heated in ways she didn't think possible.

Unfortunately, as much as she wanted to replay the events and tack on her own fantasies, there was too much work to be done.

Since the lunch rush seemed to be under control, Stella headed toward the front desk. Checkout time had passed an hour ago and they were due to get a new wave of couples. Every room was booked, which was always a good thing on a weeknight.

Since Stella had taken over, she'd been trying her hardest to make sure her marketing team kept pumping out information and waving the amenities around all over social media. The previous manager hadn't been interested in growing the business, but rather staying behind his desk and remaining stagnant. All he cared about was that he got paid.

Well, that had put a damper on her father's plans to watch cash just flood in, so Stella had jumped at the chance to not only manage this remarkable resort, but also show her father she was a worthy businesswoman.

She didn't need his approval. She didn't need his money. But she wanted his respect and she had a sickening feeling in her gut that she'd never get it.

This was her last chance. She was done putting herself out there, basically waving around in his face all the ways that she was worthy to be in his world, his damn life. If he didn't acknowledge her or treat her the way she deserved, then she'd be done.

Even if that would leave her officially alone. Over time she had come to the realization that perhaps she'd be better off alone than begging for attention or love from her own father.

Stella passed through the wide-open, four-story lobby. She never tired of the beauty of this place. Not only had Mirage been built with wood from the forest where the building stood, the place had been built around some of the old trees. Literally, there was a large, live ponderosa pine growing straight up through the middle of the lobby. It was quite a focal point for newcomers looking for a place to take selfies.

Besides the live trees randomly found inside the resort, there were windows absolutely everywhere. A breathtaking view was never farther than a glance in one direction or the other. Mountain views were the main reason Stella loved not staying behind her desk. She'd taken the smallest office, though she had a feeling her father had a hand in doling that area out to her.

Even though she was rushing from one crisis to another, at least she was surrounded by breathtaking splendor, so she wasn't about to complain.

After Stella registered several people, she headed toward her office just to double-check on the couples currently on fantasy dates. No matter what the couple wanted, the discreet employees at Mirage worked overtime to make it happen.

In the short time she'd been there, she'd had some strange requests and some...risqué ones, as well. It was not her place to judge or try to understand people's fetishes, but she had to admit sometimes she was intrigued.

And that intrigue only intensified when the thought of Dane Michaels flooded her mind. She couldn't help but wonder what he'd think if she invited him to the Lumberjack Room or the Campfires and Corsets Room. No doubt she'd be in over her head, but part of her wanted to. She ached to get his hands on her.

But there would be no need for fantasy dates between her and the sexy rancher in the penthouse. That man was already like every single sexy dream she'd ever had come to life. If she wanted to try something daring, risky, adventurous, she had a feeling just sleeping with that man would embody all three.

Stella smoothed her hair behind her ears and let out a sigh as she rounded her desk. She didn't bother taking a seat, there was never any time for such things. She cross-referenced her lists of guests and their requests, feeling reassured in her certainty that her staff could handle every need that was requested and any additional ones coming in.

Well, food and fantasies were covered for the next twenty-four hours. Maybe she would get through this day without a complete meltdown or catastrophe. One could hope.

Stella rounded her desk to head back out, but Dane filled her doorway and she froze in place. Her hand rested on the mahogany desk and her toes curled in her boots.

"Didn't think you'd be someone stuck in an office."

He hooked his thumbs through his belt loops and steadied those dark eyes right on hers…right after he gave her a visual sampling. Perhaps the sampling he'd had last night hadn't been enough.

Her eyes were drawn to that belt buckle again. She'd ask him about the emblem sometime, though she already knew he'd tell her that it was his ranch. She found that she genuinely wanted to know more about it…about him.

"I'm rarely in here," Stella replied, attempting to get her heart rate and nerves to settle. "I had a few things to check on. How did you know where my office was?"

The offices and anything considered "behind the scenes" were discreetly hidden from guests. Lara had thought of everything when she'd designed the adult retreat. She'd wanted the guests to feel like they were truly in a magical place and reality didn't exist.

Dane shrugged and offered that sexy, borderline naughty half grin. "I can be persuasive when I want something."

Wasn't that the truth. She wasn't naive enough to ask him what he wanted from her. He'd made that perfectly clear last night. In his defense, she'd also made her own wants quite apparent, even if she hadn't fully acted on them.

"Dane—"

Her cell rang from inside the pocket of her button-up plaid dress. She held up a hand to Dane. "I need to take this."

He nodded, but didn't step out to give her privacy. Instead, he actually came on in and made himself at home by going straight to the window to look out over the back of the property.

Stella smiled at his audacity, but pulled her ringing phone out. One look at the screen and that smile vanished. She resisted the urge to groan or flat-out ignore the call, but she reminded herself that she wanted this. She wanted a relationship, so she swiped her finger across the screen.

"Dad," she greeted. "I haven't heard from you for a while. How are you?"

"I've been busy working." The gruff reply wasn't abnormal or unexpected. "Have you been keeping an eye on the weather? There's a storm coming and they're saying it could be quite substantial."

Storms in Montana were always substantial. They were in the mountains so high, they were about one good stretch from touching clouds—or so it seemed most days. Snow and blizzards were nothing new here. And of course she kept her eye on the weather. Just like everything else around here. She had to stay sharp and know everything going on inside and out of her resort. Well…almost her resort.

"I'm aware," she replied, risking a glance to Dane who remained with his back to her. "Everything is under control, Dad. Our backup systems have never failed and all of our guests will remain comfortable and happy. We're actually booked up for the next month."

She couldn't help the pride that surged through her. When she'd come on board, they hadn't been completely booked up, which told her that her marketing team had tapped into something brilliant in a relatively short time.

"Only a month ahead?" he scoffed.

Stella gritted her teeth and turned to pace to the other end of the office. There was no way Dane wasn't hearing every word she said, but she couldn't focus on the handsome stranger right now.

"In comparison to last year, we're doing a remarkable job," she retorted. "It's been years since Mirage has been completely booked for more than a night at a time."

When her father had first purchased the resort, he'd had an amazing manager, but when that manager passed away suddenly, her father had scrambled to fill the spot. Unfortunately, the replacement lasted only a year and that had been enough time to see numbers start to decline.

So here she was cleaning up someone else's mess all while proving to her father that she was capable and deserved to have this property.

"One month of solid bookings won't make up for three years of dismal numbers," he replied.

"Yes, well, I'm working as hard as I can." If he was here, perhaps he'd see that. "I'm confident the numbers will continue to grow now that I'm in charge."

"And what have you done about the chef who quit?"

Of course he would know about that. He wasn't a ruthless businessman for nothing. He'd never let his investments go unsupervised—and he wouldn't consider his daughter to be supervision enough on her own. Stella had no doubt her father had spies strategically placed throughout the resort, either as employees or guests.

Dread curled through her. She'd just been half joking to herself, imaging the resort full of spies, but now that she thought about it, she realized she wouldn't put it past him. In fact, she was positive he'd done just that. There was no other way he would know about the chef less than twenty-four hours after the man quit.

"Like I said, I have everything under control," she told him.

On a sigh, she spun back around, only to lock eyes on Dane. She hadn't seen that look from him before...something akin to compassion or worry. But just as quick as she saw it, the look vanished.

"If you want to know more about what's going on here, you can ask me or maybe come check things out yourself. I think you'd be pleasantly surprised," she added. "But I don't appreciate being spied on."

Her breath caught in her throat as she continued to stare at Dane. "I have to go," she told her dad before disconnecting the call.

Without taking her eyes from Dane, she slid her phone back into her pocket then crossed her arms.

"How long have you been working for my father?"

Dane's dark brows rose toward his hairline. "Excuse me?"

"You were sent here to spy on me, right? See if I can actually do this job and not screw it up?"

She'd been such a fool to think a kind stranger just happened upon her and saved the day, then was suddenly attracted to her.

"Does he know you want to sleep with me or is

that all part of his plan?" Stella asked, suddenly sickened at the idea. "How much is he paying you?"

Before she could draw her next breath, Dane had closed the distance between them. His fingers curled around her biceps and he hauled her against his chest. The motion had her tipping her head back to keep her focus on him.

"You think I'd whore myself out?" he demanded. "I don't work for anybody and I sure as hell wouldn't take money to have sex with you."

Oh, he was angry. She didn't know Dane, but after hearing the conviction in his voice, she had no doubt he was telling the truth. Beneath that anger, Stella saw pain.

"When I get you in my bed, it won't have anything to do with your father," he growled.

When.

Her entire body heated between the threatened promise of her in his bed and the way he'd plastered his body against hers from hip to chest, and Stella couldn't do a thing but hold on.

She gripped his arms and stared back into those dark eyes, now hard with fury. But she wasn't scared. Dane wouldn't hurt her. Someone who sacrificed his whole evening to help a complete stranger, expecting nothing in return, wasn't a person who should be feared.

But he was hurt by her accusation.

"I'm sorry." Stella closed her eyes and pulled in a

shaky breath, trying to rein in her frustrations. "My father… It's all complicated, but I think he's spying on me and how I'm doing here. With the timing of you showing up, I just jumped to conclusions when I shouldn't have doubted you."

Dane's grip lessened, but he didn't let her go. He eased back slightly, the muscle in his jaw clenched.

"Your father doesn't trust you?" Dane asked, his brows drawn in.

"Apparently not. I never thought that was an issue," she replied, hurt spreading through her. "But it would seem that my loyalty is in question or at least my judgment." Stella shook her head and attempted a smile. "I don't know why I find you so easy to talk to. Sorry about all that."

Dane stroked his thumbs over the curve of her shoulders. "Don't apologize. I'd say I'm easy to talk to because I don't know the dynamics here. I'm just a stranger to you."

Yes, something she needed to remind herself of. She shouldn't get wrapped up in a stranger, emotionally or physically.

Yet here she was, doing a stellar job of both.

Everyone had a breaking point and apparently Dane Michaels was hers. She'd worked so hard for so long, putting her personal life on the back burner. No, her personal life wasn't even on the stove, let alone a burner.

Maybe she should take an hour a day just for herself…and whatever pleasantries came along.

"Come to my penthouse for dinner," she told him. "I'll have everything ready at eight."

Dane's brows shot up. "You live on-site full-time?"

Stella nodded. "There's no way I'd want to commute when I'm always needed. This resort is my life, my baby. I want to always be available."

"You really do love this place," he muttered.

"Of course I do." She stepped back, needing to distance herself from the man who had her reevaluating her priorities. "So, eight o'clock?"

"You don't need to feed me dinner."

Stella smoothed her hair away from her face and squared her shoulders. "I do, so don't argue. I'll apologize and you'll be a gentleman and accept my offerings."

Once again, he got that hungry look in his eyes. Being in such close proximity with Dane made it quite difficult to remain a professional.

"Do you really think you'll be back to your room by eight?"

"I'll make it happen if you promise to be there."

Dane flashed her that smile that had her stomach tightening with anticipation. "I'll be there."

He leaned forward, not reaching for her or even attempting to touch her. His breath on the curve of her ear sent shivers assaulting her every nerve ending.

"I'm counting down the hours until I touch you again," he murmured.

Before she could regain her mental balance, Dane had eased around her and walked out of her office. Stella remained in place, wondering how she was going to focus on work when her body was more than ready for Dane's promised touch.

And just how the hell was she supposed to concentrate on the potential storm heading toward the resort when her own storm was taking over her emotions?

Six

Damn. There was nothing sexier than an aggressive, confident woman. Stella not only embodied both of those qualities, she was so much more and Dane hadn't expected her to be the complete package.

What he had expected to be a little flirting with a vulnerable woman who would give him insight to her father was turning into so much more than he ever expected.

Dane had the flirting down and was well on his way to the seduction—a little *too* well, really. Whenever he was near her, he couldn't seem to remember why taking her to bed was anything other than an excellent idea. He was drawing her in, just as he'd intended, and yet the draw pulled just as strongly on him. This woman was a force all her own.

And as far as the insight to her father? Well, Dane's original assumptions were correct. The guy was a bastard in the same over-entitled category as his own stepfather.

It was no wonder those two had done a business deal. Sharks tended to swim together. But Dane had heard a rumor the reality was that Robert had lost the resort in a gambling bet gone bad.

Never in all of his plotting and scheming did he ever think she'd assume he worked for her father. Dane hadn't lied when he told her no. He hadn't lied when he said he wouldn't whore himself out or take money for sex.

But he would take the resort.

The guilt he'd tried to ignore, the guilt he'd told himself wasn't there, suddenly grew sharp teeth and clung tight to his soul.

He'd come this far. Nothing and no one would stop him…not even Stella. He hated with every ounce that she was going to get hurt by his takeover of the resort. There was no avoiding that. But perhaps once she moved on she would see that Dane had saved her from her father. Because that man would never be happy with her running any of his businesses. Dane wasn't sure of the issues that circulated between father and daughter. That wasn't Dane's business, but that didn't stop him from wondering.

Dane left his penthouse at exactly eight and headed toward Stella's rooms on the other side of the resort. Since leaving her earlier he'd done some exploring, taking in what had been changed since his mother's passing and the last time he'd been there.

But even the remodeling, the addition with more saunas and private movie rooms in the back, the suspended decks overlooking the valley…none of that had taken his mind off the scene in Stella's office. His mind just kept circling back to the phone call he'd overheard.

What the hell kind of game was her father playing? From what Dane knew, Stella had six months to turn this resort around and pull in more money than the previous manager had lost in the past year—a manager hired by Stella's father, and kept in the position despite obvious incompetence, when her father still didn't see her as fit for the job.

Well, here she was, doing a stellar job and Ruiz Garcia still didn't see what an amazing business-woman she truly was. Dane hadn't missed the way she'd lowered her voice when he'd been present. He hadn't missed the disappointment and the hurt lacing each and every word. And he hadn't missed the pain in her eyes when she'd realized her father had likely planted a spy.

What really pissed him off was that she'd thought that was him. But he wasn't angry with her any-more—no, he was angry with himself. She had every reason to be suspicious, given the timing. But her suspicions were pointing her in the wrong direction. He *was* a spy, but the only person he worked for was himself. Dane would never work for a backstabbing mastermind like Ruiz, but could he really claim to be that much better when he was plotting against Stella even as he headed toward her for their date?

Dane made his way through the lobby and glanced out the doors into the darkened night. Snowflakes swirled around in the beams of light. The storm was rolling in and, if the forecast was correct, they were in for a hell of a blizzard.

Living in Montana had acclimated him to snow and cold. He loved the weather, actually. His ranch was postcard worthy all blanketed with snow. He longed to be back there now, to be in his den with a roaring fire and his two golden retrievers, Buck and Bronco, asleep on the rug in front of the crackling flames.

Thankfully his housekeeper was staying in the guest quarters and taking care of the dogs while his foreman oversaw everything ranch-related. Dane trusted very few people, but once they were in his inner circle, they were there for life.

As Dane passed the hallway toward the Sleepy Forest suites, he did a quick glance and spotted a couple in their midfifties, if he had to guess. They were hand in hand and staring at each other as if nobody else existed outside their happy little bubble.

Dane couldn't imagine ever letting someone that deeply into his heart. There was only so much brokenness a man could take and Dane truly felt he'd had his fair share over time. With the loss of his mother, the distance with his brother, the loss of friends in the war...

He didn't even want to pretend to play the game of feelings and emotions and hoping for a successful long-term relationship. Living on his own and worrying only about himself and his ranch was more than enough to make him happy in this life.

When he took the private elevator to Stella's penthouse, he forced himself to calm down and regain his focus. Getting wrapped up in her personal struggles with her father was definitely not Dane's place. The only reason he needed that information was to use it to obtain everything he wanted.

And the damn guilt? He couldn't get wrapped up in that, either. Not only was his brother counting on him, Dane owed this to his mother who never, ever had any intention of selling her businesses... let alone to the devil.

Stella may think she wanted to be here and manage Mirage, but until she was out from her father's thumb, would she truly be happy?

She was brilliant, she had a drive not many people had. Stella would go on to do greater things, on her own, without her father.

Ready to get this night going, Dane tapped his

knuckles on the door and waited. He didn't have to wait long. The double doors swung open and Stella stood before him looking just as stunning as she'd been this morning. Even working herself ragged, somehow she managed to come across as in control and put together.

If it hadn't been for that brief moment in her office when she'd looked so hurt while on the phone with her father, Stella would have convinced him not a thing was wrong in her world. He knew better.

The nugget of guilt grew, taking root.

"Perfect timing," she stated with a smile as she gestured him in. "I just got everything set up and sent the cook away."

Dane stepped in and instantly fell back into his past. Nostalgia hit him hard as he scanned his eyes over the open space. He'd been a preteen when his mother had opened Mirage. This had been her on-site room and Dane and Ethan would take turns getting the fire going on cold, snowy nights...just like tonight.

He swept his gaze back across the spacious room, taking in all the familiarity and noting each change since he'd been here last. Little touches made the room all Stella. The pictures across the mantel, the bright red throw over the leather chair, a pair of worn boots next to the sofa.

But so much was still the same. That stone around the fireplace he'd helped choose with his mother, the dark kitchen cabinets and raw-edged counter-tops... The leather sofas were the same, the lamps were the same, the chocolate fur rug in front of the fire was the same.

So much reminded him of his mother, which only added to his steely structure and mental drive to finish the job he'd started.

Lara had loved her boys with her entire being. She'd done all of this for them, for their future. She'd taken the inheritance from her grandfather and invested every single penny first into this resort and then, just as soon as it started showing a profit, she'd opened her second Mirage location.

Nearly twenty years had gone by since Dane had seen her or even heard her voice, but she was still here. This room, this resort, they were all pieces of her and he wasn't going to stop until he got them all back...no matter who he had to use to serve his purpose.

"You didn't have to send up wine and flowers this afternoon."

Stella's sweet voice pulled him from the tunnel of thoughts. He turned to face her just as she closed the door and leaned back against it.

"And the basket of spa and bath items was too much," she added. "But that robe and those slippers feel like heaven, so thank you."

Dane nodded. "I figured you don't take the time

to pamper yourself, so I thought you might need a reminder."

Stella pushed off the door and closed the distance between them. "I don't even know how you managed to get everything delivered to my penthouse because I know you didn't purchase the flowers from the gift shop and those lotions in the basket are from France."

"And how do you know that?" he asked.

"Because that is my favorite brand, right down to the scent." Stella crossed her arms and tipped her head. "Apparently you have some incredible resources if you could manage all of this in a short amount of time."

She didn't need to know that it took only one phone call to make all of this happen. He'd spared no expense on the items themselves and had paid another hefty sum to get everything delivered without Stella sensing a thing.

And yet he got the oddest sense that it was the fact that he'd made an effort, that he'd tried to treat her, to spoil her a little, that pleased her the most. Did she ever have anyone do something just for her? Or was she too busy worrying how to please everyone else and still reach her goals?

Ignoring her statement, because she didn't need to know just how far his reaches were, Dane took a step back and glanced toward the fireplace where a table had been set up.

"Did you order all of this or did you have them

send up some leftovers?" he asked, turning his focus back to her.

Stella's dark eyes narrowed as she swatted at him. "Leftovers? You think I invited you to my room for leftovers?"

Dane reached for her hand and had her tumbling against his chest, earning him a small squeak from her lips. She tipped her head back and met his gaze.

"What *did* you invite me here for?" he murmured, mesmerized by the thick black lashes framing her expressive eyes.

Damn it. If he wasn't careful he'd find himself lost in Stella and ignoring all the things he actually should be doing.

Like getting her to open up and trust him…

"I wanted to see you," she whispered. "To…talk."

Dane couldn't stop the twitch of his lips. "Talk? When I kissed you earlier you didn't seem so eager to talk."

"Maybe that kiss affected you more than it did me."

Dane didn't even think before he crushed his lips to hers. Like hell she wasn't affected. And so was he, whether he wanted to be or not. He'd been waiting too long for another sample. Nine whole hours and every minute that went by, he could still taste her. Well, now he didn't have to fantasize because she was in his arms.

Or more like plastered against him, which was

exactly where he wanted her. He hadn't expected to physically ache for her. Never once did he consider that he would have an issue with self-control. Dane was always in control—except when the nightmares came. But with women? When he'd gone to bed with the few women he'd had since coming home scarred and broken, he'd never relinquished his power or felt out of control.

Dane wrapped his arms around her, settling his hands over her round backside and urging her hips to align with his.

Stella let out a little moan as he coaxed her lips apart and thrust his tongue against hers. There was no hesitation on her end, and much to his surprise, she reached up with her free hand and threaded her fingers through his unruly hair. That slight tug had even more arousal pumping through him.

He turned her toward the back of the leather sofa and lifted her to sit on the top of the cushions. Dane stepped between her spread legs and raked his hands up her bare thighs and beneath the hem of her skirt.

Pulling her hand from between their bodies and out of his grip, Stella reached for the buckle on his belt and gave a swift jerk.

Dane pulled away and worked on taking deep breaths and getting this situation back under his control. He still needed information and it was damn difficult to think with her mouth all over his.

"Why don't we eat?" he suggested.

Stella blinked and dropped her hands. "Right... um, that is the reason I invited you."

"And to talk," he reminded her, because hearing all about her life with her father was of the utmost importance...despite his arousal.

Stella slid off the couch and straightened her dress. Every part of Dane wanted to finish what they'd started—but that just proved that he needed to back away. He had to stay in control, had to keep his eye on the prize and not get distracted by how good she looked. And smelled. And tasted...

Everything about Stella had become more complicated than he'd initially thought. Each moment had to be assessed and plotted.

Dane followed the sway of Stella's hips as she led the way toward the table for two set up in front of the fireplace. But when she just stood there, looking down at the setting, Dane came up beside her.

"Something wrong?"

Her eyes shifted to him and she smiled. "Let's take dinner onto the balcony."

The climate-controlled, glassed-in balcony off the bedroom would be less intimate.

"Sounds good to me."

They both filled their plates and grabbed their wineglasses before heading out to the cozy, spacious area high above the valley. This was just another area he and Ethan had enjoyed when they came to stay with their mother. They'd pretend they were military spies looking over enemy territory.

Dane glanced to the L-shaped sofa and pushed aside the memories of when the space had three plaid upholstered chairs for Ethan, their mother and Dane. Their stepfather was often out doing business, leaving the three of them alone, which had been just fine with Dane. From day one he'd had an odd feeling about the guy his mother had married, but it hadn't been until after his mother's death that that feeling had grown into full-fledged hatred.

Stella took a seat in the corner of the sofa and extended her legs out, propping her plate on her lap. Dane sat on the other end and balanced his plate on one leg and sat his wineglass on the maple table before him.

"Is this the first time this week you've made it back to your room at a reasonable time?" he asked, stabbing the steak with his fork.

"Yes." She took a sip of her wine and leaned to the side to put her glass next to his. "The first time in a lot longer than a week, actually. I've never had a reason to get back to my room by a certain time. Nothing seemed as important as being with my staff and ensuring all the guests' needs were attended to."

"I'm flattered I ranked above that," he commented.

"Oh, if I get a call, I'm heading back down," she stated with a laugh. "Nothing comes between me and my goals."

Dane shot her a side glance and found her looking back at him. Apparently he'd been added to her goal list, which was fine with him. But then the scars would come up and that wasn't exactly a point he wanted to discuss.

And yet another niggling speared at him. She had no clue why he was here, what he was capable of doing…what he would ultimately take from her.

Guilt could be all-consuming, but he had to remain focused. He had to see this through.

Dane forced his eyes back to his plate and focused on the meal. Guilt had no place here, not if he wanted to complete this mission. It wasn't his fault that she'd ended up in this situation, nor was it his duty to protect innocent people.

Dane had been innocent, too, but his life had still been ruined and he'd been left to his own devices.

None of this was what his mother would've wanted. She'd had her own plan of passing these resorts to her boys and Dane and Ethan were going to see that plan through…no matter the cost.

"This place is rather remarkable," he said after a while. "You've got to be proud of what you've done."

"I am, but it's not my opinion that matters."

"Your opinion should be the only one that matters," he countered, trying to rein in his anger. "If your father can't see how amazing you are, then maybe he's not worthy of your loyalty."

Stella set her plate on the table and grabbed her

wineglass. "I'm not sure anything can impress my father, to be honest. He sets a level of standards that no one could possibly reach."

Dane finished his meal and set his plate next to hers. He reached for his own glass and scooted down to sit next to her. Stella took another drink, then let out a clipped laugh.

"I should've learned my lesson when I was nineteen. I got the silver medal in a national competition for cross-country skiing and he was angry that I hadn't lived up to his expectations and placed first."

Dane recalled her medal mention in the background check he'd had done. He shouldn't be surprised at her father's lack of enthusiasm or praise. He didn't deserve her loyalty.

Dane knew all too well what it was like to be alone like Stella was. Having a bastard father was the same as going through life without one. While he had his brother, he and Ethan had never been the same since their mother passed, and he knew that emotional gap was partly his fault.

When he came to Mirage, Dane never expected to have so much in common with Stella, yet he found himself drawing closer to her in ways that could and would get him into trouble if he didn't stay emotionally detached.

Dane set his glass down before plucking hers from her hand and placing it back on the table. He shifted toward her, placing one hand on the cushion beside her head and the other near her hip.

"Maybe for the next several hours we forget everything outside of this room," he suggested.

Stella's eyes widened as she eased farther back onto the cushions. "Hours? You think quite a lot of yourself."

"When I get your clothes off, I intend to take my time," he promised.

He very deliberately said nothing about shedding his own clothes. Maybe there was a way they could make this work without him baring too much—of his skin or anything else. There were so many ways to make a woman feel good. Stella deserved every single one of them.

Stella's chest rose and fell with each breath. The little button at the top of her dress strained against her chest and Dane didn't take his eyes off her as he reached for the closure and freed her.

When she smiled, he slid his hand down to the next button and slid it through the slit. A flash of red lace teased him, mesmerized him. That was exactly the lingerie he'd imagined she'd be wearing. Nothing plain or simple for this bold, assertive woman. Of course she'd have red. The power color suited her.

"Are you starting that time now?" she asked, her voice breathless with want.

Dane ignored her question and slid a finger between her breasts. Such silky skin against his rough, ranch-hardened hands. He'd always been a hands-on guy—in and out of the bedroom. And he couldn't remember the last time he'd wanted to get his hands on someone this badly.

He knew he should resist. But she made it so damn hard...in all the best ways. He needed to slow this down. Regain control. Focus on what she needed, rather than what the craving in his blood demanded.

"I'm still exploring." Up, down. He continued to let his fingertip glide over her. "Trust me, you'll know when I get started."

Stella covered his hand with hers and pushed down. "I still have more buttons."

Yeah, he'd noticed. The damn dress had little buttons that went from chest to just above her knees. She'd looked like an adorable little package just waiting to be unwrapped.

He placed her hand on the next button and let go, silently urging her to continue. With a naughty smile to match the gleam in her eyes, Stella kept her focus on him as she finished revealing the rest of her curvy body.

And then a shrill ring pierced the moment.

With a groan, Stella sat up, forcing Dane back.

"I have to get that," she stated with an apologetic tone.

Dane let her up and watched as she covered her body and made her way back into the penthouse.

A large part of him wanted to take that phone and smash the hell out of it, but the other part of him, the businessman in him, understood her commitment to her work.

He'd fallen into his ranch by sheer luck. He'd purchased it during a foreclosure and made one wise investment and purchase after another. He'd worked damn hard to get where he was today.

Honestly, Dane hadn't known just how much he would appreciate Stella until he arrived and saw her in action. He'd never taken into account just how much she did for Mirage. Because of her, his mother's business was back to thriving. The resort was moving into a stronger year of sales and coming back from the brink of near financial ruin.

Dane went to the window and shoved his hands into his pockets as he looked out onto the fat flakes coming down. The storm was going to hit hard and fast. People accustomed to Montana weather wouldn't be fazed by this blizzard, but those who had traveled in from places that didn't measure snow by the foot might be in for a surprise.

The mountain would be cut off to all traffic if the storm came in as wild and ferocious as predicted.

Dane blew out a sigh and cocked his neck from side to side. Even analyzing the damn weather did nothing to squelch his arousal. He'd had Stella spread out before him, arching against his touch, and—

"I have to go."

Dane turned to see Stella pulling her hair back into a low ponytail, her dress now all buttoned back up as if nothing had ever happened. His heart rate was still accelerated and now that he knew exactly what she hid beneath that dress, he couldn't shut down quite so quickly.

"What's wrong?" he asked.

Stella turned and headed through the penthouse, pocketing her cell and charging toward the door. Dane followed behind her. "Emergency with one of the rooms. I'll tell you more later. Stay and have more to eat or…whatever."

And then she was gone.

Dane could search her entire penthouse if he wanted, but he knew there would be no hidden secrets kept here. Everything he hoped to learn would come from the tidbits he picked up from Stella herself.

And from the little time he'd spent with her, he'd learned a good bit about her father. Other than the fact Ruiz was a bastard, something Dane already knew, he also discovered there were very likely spies in place throughout Mirage, which meant Dane had to be careful.

Ruiz was stringing his daughter along, making her do his grunt work at this resort, all while waiting to bring in the extra cash.

Dane was willing to up his offer, but there had to be something he was missing. A man like Ruiz

Garcia let his entire life revolve around money. The first amount Dane proposed had been turned down flat without so much as a counter. What was it that Ruiz was holding on to? And why?

That was what Dane needed to find out and he wasn't done with Stella until he did.

Seven

After three hours of trying to calm down the newlywed couple in the Summit Suite, Stella was beyond exhausted.

She'd run out so fast on Dane that she was a little embarrassed—but she'd been nothing less than honest with him about how married she was to this place. Everything fell in line behind keeping Mirage in the best standings with each guest that came through.

Good thing she wasn't looking for a relationship because she was not the prize any man would want. Every man she knew had an ego that was too large for him to stand behind her career. That was fine with her.

Stella stepped off the elevator and crossed the

hall toward her penthouse. Once she was inside, she closed her eyes and leaned back against the door. She wasn't sure what time it was, but she knew she was dead on her feet. She also was well aware the storm outside was raging and come morning, the mountain road would likely be shut down.

One worry at a time.

"You look worn-out."

Stella startled and blinked as she focused on the man across the room. Oh, what that man could do to a simple tee and a pair of jeans.

"Dane." She pushed off the door and bent down to pull off her knee boots. "I never thought you'd still be here."

Dane remained across the room near the fireplace. Clearly he'd made himself at home because he held a tumbler of the bourbon she knew had been tucked away in a cabinet when she'd left. Stella didn't care for the stuff, but when her father came, she tried to have his favorite brand on hand.

"I wanted to make sure you were taken care of," Dane replied. He tipped back the last of his drink and crossed the room to her. "Go soak in the bath and I'll bring you a glass of wine."

Stella dropped her boots next to the door and laughed. "It's after midnight. I don't have time to sit in the tub no matter how amazing that sounds."

When he came to stand in front of her, Stella let

out a sigh and that pretty much stole the little bit of
energy she had left.

"Dane, if you came for—"

He framed her face with hands that held her so
very gently, all while looking at her like she was made
of glass. Right now, that wasn't too far from the truth.
The days were catching up with her and she was starting to worry maybe she did need help and couldn't
do this all by herself. But if she admitted any type of
weakness, her father would immediately deem her
unsuitable to run his business.

It would be the national championship all over
again. Never coming in first, always falling short.

"I knew you'd argue."

Dane's words barely registered before he bent and
picked her up. With one arm behind her back and the
other behind her knees, he headed toward the mas-
ter bath. Stella laid her head against his chest and
closed her eyes.

"You should go," she murmured. "I'll take a quick
bath to relax, but you should already be in your room
sleeping like the rest of the guests."

Dane eased her onto the edge of the Jacuzzi tub.
"If I left, you'd fall asleep in the bathtub and drown.
Now get your clothes off."

He started the water, testing it with his hand and
completely ignoring her as she started working on
each button.

"You really didn't stay for sex?" she asked, shrugging out of her dress.

Dane's focus turned to her, his dark eyes raking over her bare skin. The hunger just as apparent as when he'd been touching her earlier.

"You'll be wide-awake when I have you."

He stood straight up and glanced around the spacious bath. He went to the vanity and searched through the basket he'd had delivered, pulling out products before settling on one. He flicked the top, sniffed, seemed to nod in agreement with himself and dumped the entire bottle into the bath.

Stella laughed. "That's a bit much and one hell of an expensive bath."

He set the empty bottle back on the vanity. "I'll buy you more."

Stella couldn't wrap her mind around this guy. Who was he? Other than a perfect stranger who'd swept into her life just as fiercely as the storm threatening the mountain.

But…was Dane a threat? He hadn't shown any sign of that and she truly didn't believe he worked for her father. That idea had popped into her head due to stress and exhaustion from dealing with, well, everything.

Stella removed her bra and panties and slid into the warm bath. She didn't even try to suppress the moan as she let the heat and fragrant bubbles envelop her. She leaned back against the cushioned bath pillow and closed her eyes.

"Don't let me drown," she muttered.

Dane's chuckle carried from the room, as did his footsteps over the hardwood floor. Maybe if she just relaxed for a few minutes and let someone else take care of her she could revive herself.

Letting someone else have control certainly wasn't the norm for her. Since her mother passed during childbirth, Stella had spent her whole life figuring out how to take care of herself.

Her father often blamed her for her mother's death. He punished her with a strict childhood that always kept Stella in line. By the time she was a teen, she realized that he was an angry, bitter man, lashing out over the loss of his wife. Being left with a daughter when he'd wanted a son hadn't helped matters.

Still, he was the only parent she knew and she wanted…something. At first she wanted acceptance, then she wanted acknowledgment. Now…

Stella opened her eyes and blinked against the burn. She hadn't cried in so long and she certainly didn't like feeling so vulnerable. But was it too much to ask to just be loved by a parent? Was she that hard to accept and let in?

"Here you go." Dane strode back into the room and set the stemless wineglass on the edge of the garden tub. "Oh, no."

He stared down at her as he took a seat next to her glass. "Why the tears?"

Dane reached out and swiped the pad of his thumb over her cheeks and Stella's heart thumped. She'd known him such a short time, yet she felt some strange connection to him, yet she truly didn't know him all that well.

"It's just been a long day," she replied, offering a smile. "The bath does help and the wine is a definite perk."

"I'm not sure how much this is helping if you're upset." He cocked his head and continued to look at her with worry etched over his ruggedly handsome face. "I only stepped out for a minute."

Stella curled her fingers around her wineglass and lifted it to her lips. Bubbles slid down her arm and dripped back into the water. She let the cool, crisp, fruity blend calm her and make her think of happier times. There were happy times…weren't there?

"Have you ever wanted something so badly, living your whole life for that moment when you'd get it, but once you got there, you realized maybe you're just a fool and it was never in your reach at all?"

She was babbling, she knew, but she risked a glance at Dane and noted the sympathy had turned to understanding and maybe a dose of anger. The muscle in his jaw clenched and he merely offered a clipped nod.

"I don't know that I'll ever be what my father

wants," she went on. "I'm not sure *I* want to be, honestly. I'll never understand how he couldn't just love me for me. Why we can't just be father and daughter. But after all this time, it's just not going to happen. Is it?"

She shouldn't have tacked on that question, but part of her wanted him to counter and tell her she was mistaken. She wanted someone on her team, in her corner, cheering her on. Damn it. When did she get so wimpy and weak?

"I don't know your father," Dane stated slowly as if choosing his words carefully. "But I do know we don't always get great parents. My mother was the best. She raised my brother and me as a single mom and we were always her top priority. Then she remarried and my stepfather was…well, he wasn't parent material. When she passed, we were stuck with him and that's when we realized what a true bastard he was."

Stella set her glass on the edge and sat up in the water. Dane's eyes instantly went to her chest and her body immediately responded.

"Sounds like we both had to pave our own way."

Dane reached into the water, keeping his eyes on hers the entire time. "You're not relaxing."

His hand found her thigh. That firm grip held her for a moment before he trailed his fingers up. Stella instinctively spread her legs and let her head fall back against the bath pillow.

"Drink your wine," he demanded in that husky tone dripping with arousal. "I've got this."

Stella reached for her glass, but had to hold it with two hands to prevent herself from dropping it into the bubbles as those clever fingers parted her. Stella took a sip, her eyes locking on Dane's over the top of her glass.

That dark unruly hair, the heavy-lidded gaze, the black stubble along his jawline all joined together to give him that mysterious, alluring factor. She'd never been reckless with anything in her life, let alone with her body. She'd been too focused on work, on moving forward to prove herself.

Letting a near stranger touch her this way felt wrong…yet oh so right.

Dane slid one finger into her and Stella arched her back, biting her lip to keep from crying out. As wave after wave of pleasure slid over her, she closed her eyes and let the moment capture every bit of her.

Nothing existed but Dane's touch. She gripped her glass and clutched it against her bare chest. Water rippled, almost providing soft music to frame the intimate moment. She hadn't expected this, hadn't known he'd still be here when she came home.

As her body jerked, the wine sloshed from the glass and over her chest.

Suddenly the glass disappeared from her hands and Stella focused her attention to Dane. He'd leaned down, his free hand resting on the ledge beside her head. His other hand continued to work her and her hips rose to meet each pump.

Dane dipped his head and ran his tongue along the trail of wine. He made a satisfied purring noise low in his throat. "I never thought I'd crave white wine, but damn. That's good."

He slid his lips along the path again and took his time, quite the opposite of the frantic movement of his hand beneath the bubbles.

Once the wine was gone, he lifted his head and simply watched her. Watched her as if this would be enough to satisfy him.

Stella had never been on display like this, never realized how arousing it could be to have someone watch you so intently with such determination and fixation in their eyes.

The touch, the stare, the intensity of being utterly consumed by a man she barely knew…it all became too much.

Stella reached up and curled her fingers around Dane's biceps, her other hand went to his wrist beneath the water. She didn't know if she wanted to help him or if she just didn't know where else to put her hand, but the way his muscles and tendons were flexing beneath her touch, working so hard at bringing her pleasure, had her body spiraling out of control.

Bursts of euphoria pulsed through her, her entire body tightened around him, and he murmured something as he leaned down and captured her lips. Every part of her continued to quiver as the release flowed.

Dane consumed her, but still, she wanted more.

Stella's body started to settle, leaving her sated, exhausted, and most definitely relaxed.

When she regained control of her breathing and returned to reality, Stella opened her eyes. Dane's hand rested on her thigh and that cockeyed smile matched the hunger in his eyes.

"Ready for bed?"

Stella started to sit up.

"Not sex," he added. "I already told you that's not why I'm here."

Confused, she stood, her legs trembling more than she'd expected. "Then what do you call this?"

In that slow, easy manner of his, Dane rose to his feet and reached toward the heated towel bar. He pulled off a fluffy white towel and with an expert flick, he wrapped it around her.

"I call this getting you to relax and maybe being a bit selfish in taking what I want, too." He shrugged and clutched the towel together between her breasts. "I'm human."

Her eyes darted down to just below his silver belt buckle. "I see that and you're also miserable."

"After what I just saw?" He smiled even wider and shook his head as he scooped her up and out of the tub. "I'm far from miserable. Turned on and aroused? Absolutely. But watching you like that is something I'll never forget."

Yeah, she wouldn't forget it, either. Dane had a touch like none other…at least none she'd ever had. Those rough hands could certainly do more than run a ranch—or whatever it was he did.

Mercy's sake. She'd just let a man she barely knew pleasure her in such an erotic way. When did she become that woman?

Stella rested her head against his shoulder. Perhaps she'd always been that woman—the type who deserved more than she allowed herself to have, the type who should take more of what she wanted out of life and not work herself to death, and the type who knew when a fling was too good to turn down.

"I really can't sleep long," she murmured.

As he carried her, a wave of dizziness overcame her. The hours on her feet, the warmth from the bath, the lethargy from the greatest orgasm she'd ever had…everything made her feel as if she was caught in that world between being asleep and awake.

"Stay." The single word slipped from her mouth before she could stop herself. "I don't want to be alone."

She cringed at her own words. That sounded like begging and after coming undone all around him a moment ago, she'd better watch out or he'd think she was getting attached. There was no room in her life for attachments.

Honestly, she wouldn't know how to do a relationship or commitment anyway. It wasn't as if she'd grown up with a good example. Stella wasn't sure she could ever have a normal or real relationship. Most little girls dreamed of their wedding day, but she'd only dreamed of the day her father wrapped his arms around her and told her how proud he was of her.

Tears pricked her eyes again as Dane settled her onto her bed. Before she rolled over, she thought she felt a dip on the mattress behind her.

He'd stayed. After giving so freely of his passion, expecting nothing in return, and after she'd accused him of horrible things earlier…he'd stayed. For her.

Eight

Dane stared out into the darkness. Swirling snow-flakes fluttered through the soft beam of light coming off the patio. He did his best thinking in the middle of the night, in this stretch of time when the world seemed to be calm.

After his years in the military, sleeping never came easy. Nightmares plagued him night after night, but he figured that would forever be an issue. In truth, it didn't seem to be as bad lately. He didn't know if his memories were getting better or if he'd just grown accustomed to living with the horror that was his new normal.

Dane glanced over his shoulder toward the king-size bed. The navy sheets and duvet were all twisted on one side where he'd tried to rest, but perfectly placed on the other where Stella slept beneath them.

And that sight right there perfectly summed up their differences. He was restless and edgy, never quite feeling settled with anything in his life...not since his mother's death. One would think after nearly twenty years he would find some calm center inside of himself, but one life event had rolled into another and Dane had never quite found his inner peace.

Now that Dane had a bit more insight to Stella, he had to assume she never had, either. Perhaps she didn't even know she was chasing a dream that would leave her only broken and angry.

Dane hadn't lied when he said he didn't know her father, but he was well aware the type of man Ruiz was. It didn't take much digging to find out the guy wasn't the most honest and loyal to his associates or with business deals. He looked out only for one person...himself.

So where would that leave Stella? Her father treated her like nothing more than a piece on a chessboard... and then Dane came along and did the same thing.

Guilt clawed at him as he turned his attention back to the blizzard raging outside. He caught his reflection in the darkened part of the window and muttered a curse.

How the hell did he obtain his ultimate goal and

not run over Stella in the process? That's not what his mother would have wanted. She hadn't raised them to be selfish and scheming. Yet here he was, excelling at both.

He hadn't expected to care about what was going on with Stella's personal life. When he'd planned and plotted all of this to get Mirage back, he'd only had his family in mind. Somehow, he wanted to get back what he and his brother were supposed to have and if gaining back the two resorts pushed them closer together, then that was just another reason to keep moving forward.

No matter who stood in his way.

Rustling sheets had him glancing over his shoulder. Stella sat up, the duvet pooled at her waist, her breasts on display and her midnight-black hair all around her shoulders.

The crackling fire sent a glow throughout the open room, putting out a romantic ambience that shouldn't affect him, but had his body stirring as he made his way toward the bed.

Stella raked her gaze over his bare chest. When he'd gotten up, he'd removed his shirt, but kept his jeans on. He'd like to blame his lack of sleep on the confining garment, but the truth was that PTSD and the guilt over his current situation were gnawing at him.

When she eased the covers aside and swung her legs over the bed, Dane stopped. She came to her feet and without a care to her nakedness, she crossed to him. That curvy body approached him and had his arousal pumping.

Her bare feet left whispered sounds as she seemed to glide across the wood floor. There was something so mystifying, so captivating about this woman. That was the only explanation for why he kept allowing himself to be pulled in deeper.

He'd set out to seduce her, but somewhere along the way, the roles had reversed.

Without a word, Stella reached out as she came to stand before him. Her fingertip went to the tattoo of the eagle on his chest that crept over his shoulder. His muscles tensed beneath her touch and he clenched his fists at his sides to keep from picking her up and taking her back to bed, finally having what his body craved.

Those fingertips left the ink and started traveling downward. His abs tightened as he kept his eyes locked on hers.

"Stella," he growled in warning.

The warning was more for himself, though. If he ultimately went through with this seduction, he would be just as much of a bastard as the men he hated.

Her fingers went to the snap on his jeans, pulling it loose. The zipper slid down next.

Damn it. He was human with temptation staring him right in the face. He wanted her too badly to care if it made him a bastard.

Something snapped, likely his sanity, but he circled her waist with his hands and lifted her against him. Dane crushed his mouth to hers and Stella opened for him as she wrapped her arms around his shoulders and her legs around his waist.

Dane wanted to completely consume her, to strip away everything—the clothes, the lies. The damn world outside. He wanted every bit of it gone.

Taking long strides, he headed toward the bed. He wasn't waiting any longer. Guilt had no place in business…or the bedroom. Only desire belonged here. And he desired the hell out of her. From her pants and moans and the way her fingertips dug into him, she was just as achy.

When he reached the post at the end of the bed, Dane eased her down to her feet. She blinked up at him, but he took a step back. He continued to watch her as he rid himself of his jeans and boxer briefs.

Dane stepped out of his things and kicked them aside.

"Turn around," he demanded. He couldn't risk her seeing his back, but if she wanted to believe he just enjoyed this position, that was perfectly fine… because he did.

Stella quirked a brow before obeying. Dane shifted behind her and slid his hands down her arms until he reached her wrists. He circled her delicate skin and lifted her hands, wrapping them around the thick, wood bedpost.

Dane tucked his body up against hers as he trailed his lips across her shoulder, up her neck, to the curve of her ear.

"Hold on."

He quickly grabbed a condom from his wallet and covered himself as he stepped in behind her once again. With his hands gripping her hips, he pressed his body into hers.

"Spread your legs," he murmured.

Stella stepped wider and Dane used the opportunity to ease his hand to the front of her body, pleased to discover she was more than ready to take him. He slid the tips of his fingers through her, fighting the staggering need to take this final step.

"Dane."

His name coming off her lips in a cry of pleasure was all the motivation he needed. Dane slid into her and had her crying out once again. He, on the other hand, stilled.

She. Was. Perfect.

Closing his eyes against any emotions other than lust and raw, primal need, Dane concentrated on just how amazing they were together. For this night, and maybe the duration of his stay, he wanted to be here in her bed. And out of her bed? Well, that was a space he couldn't think about right now.

Stella's knuckles whitened as she gripped the post. Her head fell back against his shoulder. As Dane continued to pump his hips, he kept his hands firmly on her thighs, his fingertips digging in to keep her in place.

He leaned down and sucked on that curve of her neck, earning him another pleasure-filled groan. Damn if he didn't know her body already and that was one of the most powerful tools he had in his arsenal.

Stella reached up higher on the post and sank back against him even farther. Within seconds she was coming undone and panting his name. Dane couldn't hold back another second and he was done trying. He followed her release, pressing his forehead against her shoulder as he gritted his teeth. He held on to her until both of their bodies ceased trembling and even then, he didn't let go.

"I think my legs are going to give out." Stella's breathless words broke the silence. "I don't know how we're still standing."

He nipped at that curve in her neck again, suddenly realizing he liked that spot because each time he touched her there, she trembled. He liked having that control over her, just that little kernel that was all his.

"We're still standing because I wasn't about to miss a second of this sweet body by falling down," he countered.

Dane spun her around and lifted her up before circling the bed and laying her back down on her side. He rested a hand on either side of her head and stared down at her dark eyes, that midnight hair spread all around her.

A sheen of sweat had broken out on her chest and Dane couldn't resist. He leaned down and took one breast into his mouth. How could he want her again when his body hadn't even recovered from the last time?

When she arched against him and let out something akin to a purr, he knew exactly how. Stella Garcia was magnetic and there was no way he could say no or deny either of them what they both needed.

"You're not going to get any more sleep."

She smiled up at him. "Is that a threat?"

He palmed the other breast. "No. That's a promise."

Nine

She didn't know how she was doing it, but somehow Stella was going from one part of the resort to another, checking on staff, guests, food, and anything else she could. She tried to stay calm and competent, but it was much more of a struggle than usual. This storm was raging like nothing she'd ever seen and she was running on next to no sleep.

And yet in spite of that, the memories from last night had her smiling as she made quick strides to one of the theater rooms. If the power went due to the blizzard, she knew her generators would kick in and there would be no worries. But she still wanted to make sure everything was in good shape and that all of her guests were as comfortable as possible. They'd likely be stuck beyond their projected date, so she planned on offering discounts and extras to make up for their inconvenience.

As much as she hated the idea of stranded guests, Stella couldn't help but feel a little giddy about one guest in particular.

Once she checked on the theater rooms and the fantasy suites, she breathed a sigh of relief. So far this day was going better than most. Each guest was quite understanding of the fact the mountain road would likely close. Each guest was also given the choice to check out now and get a discount on their next stay or continue their vacation at a lower rate. Everyone had decided to stay and she couldn't help but feel a burst of pride. Thankfully they had just enough rooms and they were full.

She was actually doing this. She was kicking ass at being the manager of Mirage, one of the most spectacular adult resorts in the world.

Stella hoped like hell whoever her father had planted here saw that. She only wished she knew who the culprit was, but she wasn't wasting her time trying to find out. Whoever it was, there was nothing she'd be doing any differently even if she knew. Her guests always came first and losing sleep, skipping meals, and having achy arches in her feet were all worth it to have happy guests.

Stella pulled her cell from her pocket to check

"FAST FIVE" READER SURVEY

Your participation entitles you to:
✴ 4 Thank-You Gifts Worth Over $20!

Complete the survey in minutes.

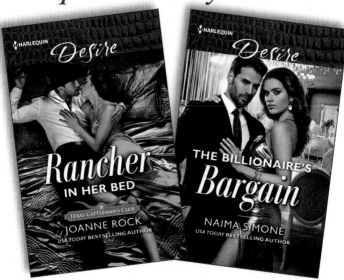

Get 2 FREE Books

See inside for details.

Dear Reader,

Since you are a lover of our books, your opinions are important to us... and so is your time.

That's why we made sure your **"FAST FIVE" READER SURVEY** can be completed in just a few minutes. Your answers to the five questions will help us remain at the forefront of women's fiction.

And, as a thank-you for participating, we'd like to send you **4 FREE THANK-YOU GIFTS!**

Enjoy your gifts with our appreciation,

Pam Powers

To get your
4 FREE THANK-YOU GIFTS:

✳ Quickly complete the "Fast Five" Reader Survey
and return the insert.

"FAST FIVE" READER SURVEY

1 Do you sometimes read a book a second or third time? ○ Yes ○ No

2 Do you often choose reading over other forms of entertainment such as television? ○ Yes ○ No

3 When you were a child, did someone regularly read aloud to you? ○ Yes ○ No

4 Do you sometimes take a book with you when you travel outside the home? ○ Yes ○ No

5 In addition to books, do you regularly read newspapers and magazines? ○ Yes ○ No

YES! I have completed the above Reader Survey. Please send me my 4 FREE GIFTS (gifts worth over $20 retail). I understand that I am under no obligation to buy anything, as explained on the back of this card.

225/326 HDL GNQC

FIRST NAME   LAST NAME

ADDRESS

APT.#   CITY

STATE/PROV.   ZIP/POSTAL CODE

READER SERVICE—Here's how it works:

the radar once again. Not that anything had changed since she looked at it thirty minutes ago, but she just wanted to see…just in case.

The bright blue blob right over Gold Valley stared back at her. Okay, well, she would get through this. Blizzards were expected in this part of the country and there wasn't much she could do to fight Mother Nature. If the mountain closed, at least her guests would be safe right here and she would play the dutiful host and make sure each need was met.

Perhaps she could include her own needs in that mix. Her cell vibrated in her hand and she glanced back down to see her father's number.

Quickly swiping the screen, she answered, "Hello."

"Stella. How are things with my resort?"

His resort. She didn't roll her eyes, but she just barely suppressed herself.

"Every room is still full and the guests are all staying through the storm."

"Of course they are. Why would they leave?"

No reason to give her any credit. Really, no problem.

"I will be arriving in two weeks to check things out," he went on. "I trust the penthouse will be ready for me."

Stella gripped the cell. "We are booked up. I wasn't aware you wanted a room."

"You don't think you should always have a handful of rooms at the ready for special clients or your own father?"

Stella smiled at a young couple strolling through the hallway. Once they passed, she still lowered her voice as she made her way toward her office.

"I think that every client deserves the same treatment no matter their financial status," she stated. "I wouldn't turn someone away in the hopes that some millionaire needed a room. I maximize on every profit possible."

"That line of thinking will get my doors closed," he growled. "If you're running my resort, then you'll do it my way."

Stella finally slipped into her office and closed the door at her back. Fury pumped through her.

"*Your* resort. *Your* way." The words slowly slipped through gritted teeth. "And here I was under the impression this resort would eventually be mine."

"That's my call and for now, Mirage is still mine. I'm sure in the next two weeks you will figure out a way to have my suite available."

"You can stay in mine," she offered. "I'll sleep on the sofa."

"Don't be absurd."

Stella took a seat in her chair and immediately realized her mistake. Now that she was down, she didn't want to get back up.

"If someone cancels, I'll be sure to put your name on that room," she promised. "But for now I need to go unless there's something else you needed."

"There is one more thing."

Stella's eyes scanned the security cameras at the front desk, the lobby, the public decks, and the front entrance. The security cameras in her office had all angles of the resort, save for the suites and the fantasy rooms.

"What's that?" she asked.

"I was offered a great deal of money to sell."

Stella's heart clenched, her breath caught in her throat and she stilled, afraid to move, desperately praying she'd heard wrong.

"I've turned the would-be buyer down," he added. There was something akin to gloating and arrogance to his tone. "But I've been wondering if you'd rather have a nest egg than a business. You could always take the money and invest, travel around the world, or even start up your own place."

Stella rested her elbows on her desk and rubbed her forehead as she pulled in a shaky breath. So that's what all of this was. Everything in his life was still about money. He'd never change, likely he never intended to give her this property. But that wouldn't stop her from pushing forward and making sure her reputation remained impeccable.

She owed that to the single mom who'd started this. A strong woman who had a vision, a passion. Stella might not have much in common with Lara as far as family life went, but she understood drive and determination.

"I don't want the money," she explained. "At the

end of this six-month experiment, I want the resort. I know I'm not the son you wanted, or the perfect business partner, but I've never given up on us."

She bit her lip the second she realized it was quivering and she was close to losing it.

"I just want a chance," she stated, once she got control of her emotions. "I've tried for so long to please you. What will it take?"

Silence on the other end had her glancing to the screen to make sure they were still connected.

"I never said you didn't please me," her father finally said. "And rehashing the past won't change a thing."

"Rehashing the past? You mean discussing my mom? Because anytime I try to talk about her, you shut the topic down."

"Stella, I will not discuss this now," he reprimanded. "I believe you have things to do. I will see you in two weeks."

He disconnected the call, leaving her emotions in even more of a jumbled mess than before. She hadn't meant to bring up her mom, but sometimes it just happened. She'd always wondered about her, wanted to see photos of her, hear stories about what she'd been like. But there had been nothing. No photos, no stories. Ruiz had shut completely down.

How did the man deal with grief or pain if he never faced it?

Laying her phone down, Stella ran her hands over

her face and took long, slow breaths to calm herself down. Leaving her office upset was not in keeping with the professional front she wanted anyone to see.

She smoothed her hair back from her face and started to stand, but stilled when she spotted Dane on the screen. He was actually outside on one of the covered patio areas. He wore a pair of jeans and a thick, wool coat. He was talking on his cell and staring out at the swirling snow. Whoever he was talking to had him shaking his head and gesturing with his free hand.

This was none of her business. She had no real ties to him, no reason to expect to be allowed some insight into his life. Yet she continued to stare. When he raked a hand over the back of his neck, Stella sank back into her chair and wondered who or what had him so upset. This wasn't the laid-back man who had pleasured her multiple times. This certainly wasn't the guy who had a life motto of "it will all work out."

She'd seen only the very sexy, very giving side of Dane Michaels. Who was he really? A rancher and ex-military, but that's all she knew.

On the screen she watched as he ended the call and pocketed his cell. Realizing she'd been staring for quite a while, Stella grabbed her own phone and came to her feet. Lunch had just passed and she hadn't grabbed a bite. She'd swing through the kitchen, make sure they were all set for dinner and the wine and cheese hour and pick something up for herself really quickly.

Maybe she should go ahead and plan a dinner for her room again. They had nowhere else to go and she wanted to take time for herself. If her father was seriously making a visit in a couple weeks, Stella was taking her reward now for the headache she'd have later.

Her cell chimed again, this time a text from the employee who kept the private hot tub areas maintained between guests.

Apparently the guests were requesting a special bottle of pinot noir and not the regular house white that was kept in that area.

Stella went to grab a bottle of the preferred wine. She of all people knew the importance of wine and a nice relaxing soak.

And once again, even in work, her mind circled back to Dane. What was she going to do when his time here came to an end?

Ten

Ethan stared at the phone and wondered what he'd said to make Dane so angry. His brother wasn't one to let his emotions drive him…or he never had been. Had that changed? Considering they hadn't spent too much time together in the past, oh, couple of decades, Ethan couldn't really consider himself an authority on his brother anymore.

All Ethan had said was that if Robert showed up at Mirage in Sunset Cove, then Ethan wasn't sure he could wait for Dane to tie up loose ends and get down there to join him. They'd waited all this time, years, to build up their resources, their finances, their power. The time to strike was now and there wasn't a chance in hell Ethan was going to let Robert slip out of their grasp again.

Ethan didn't mention that he happened to already be at Mirage. Dane thought he was just in California, but Ethan figured he should keep his plans to himself. He trusted his brother—even with the distance between them, there was no one he trusted more than Dane. They may have grown apart, but they would always have a bond like nothing else in the world. But that didn't mean his brother needed to know everything.

Shoving his cell back into the pocket of his shorts, Ethan strolled out of the open lobby area and straight toward the beach. While he was waiting on dear ol' stepdad to make his appearance, there was no reason he couldn't take in the sights while he waited... and by sights he meant that sexy, lush lady sporting a red bikini. Suddenly he had a new favorite color.

Who said he couldn't enjoy himself while on the hunt for Robert? Besides, Ethan planned on being at Mirage for a while—like forever.

As soon as he secured this place in his name, as his mother had originally intended, he planned on living right here where he belonged to manage the place and keep it prosperous. The beach, the ocean, they were home. Ethan may have grown up in Montana, but there was nothing like that salty breeze and the sand between his toes.

And the views. Had he mentioned that already?

Because he never could understand why anyone would rather be bundled up around a fire when they could be showing off sun-kissed skin and enjoying their favorite beachside beverage.

The lady in red sprayed herself with sunscreen and tossed her bottle back in her striped beach bag. He glanced up and down the shoreline. With this as an adults-only resort, there was a peacefulness not many beaches had. There were no screaming, running children since this was a private island.

Family vacations were great, but Mirage was not that type of destination. His mother, a lifelong romantic, had built two stellar resorts all with couples in mind. Her sense of romance had led to her commercial success, but also her personal downfall. She'd wanted to marry for love, she'd wholeheartedly believed in it, and she had married…but Ethan highly doubted love had entered anywhere in that equation.

Her father had passed and Lara had been left raising two boys on her own. The scenario seemed to be tailor-made for Robert because he obviously preyed on the weak and vulnerable.

The Michaels boys were neither weak nor vulnerable now. They were angry, they were still hurt, and they were ready to fight back. There was nothing Ethan wouldn't do to honor his mother, and she'd raised strong boys. This was what she would've wanted.

Ethan slipped off his flip-flops and looped his

fingers around the straps as he made his way across the warm sand.

Walking along the edge of the water always relaxed him, always helped him see a clearer picture. That was why he'd come out to Mirage instead of waiting. He needed to be here to sort through all the mess in his head, to figure out the precise steps he needed to take. He had to act fast, but he also had to be smart about it.

The sexy, curvaceous woman in red glanced his way and Ethan didn't even try to hide his smile… and he didn't move when she made her way over. A woman who knew what she wanted was one of the sexiest qualities.

Considering her smile widened as she crossed the sand toward him, well, apparently they wanted the same thing.

"I'm sorry, sir. Who did you say you were again?"

Dane didn't fault the young male for questioning the stranger who was in the midst of checking on the generators in the maintenance area. No guest should know where this room was, as rooms dedicated to the staff or the maintenance of the resort were hidden from the guests.

The entire resort had the illusion of running on fairy dust or some other magical oddity. That had been imperative to his mother who wanted couples who came here to only see the perfection, the fantasy, the beauty. "Real life" shouldn't exist on vacation, she'd always said. And she was correct. People wanted to get away from all cares and responsibilities, and she provided exactly what patrons wanted.

"Dane Michaels," he stated again as he settled his hands on his hips. "Miss Garcia asked me to check on this and she said you might be down as well since you're so thorough with your job."

The BS just rolled off his tongue, but hit the mark as the twentysomething puffed his chest with pride.

"I wasn't aware we had a new maintenance guy," the other man said. "But I checked on these yesterday."

Dane wasn't about to get into an argument or contradict the guy's mistaken assumption. But Dane would feel better if he checked on all of the "behind the scenes" things himself. After all, he had to keep up with all sides of his property.

"The storm closed the mountain." Dane purposely dodged the questioning stare from the other guy. "It's not going to let up for a few days. These generators will likely be put to use very soon."

The worker nodded. "That's what I was thinking, too."

The radio clipped to his hip crackled and a female voice came over the airwaves. He knew that voice and she may not like knowing he was in here checking things out. He listened as she requested any available hands to get to the dining area to set up for the lunch crowd.

With the storm, so many employees were unable to make their shifts, which meant the ones stuck here were pulling overtime for the foreseeable future.

And that meant Stella would be running from one end of Mirage to the other, taking little time for herself—if any. He'd make sure his mother's resort was running just fine, the guests were happy, and Stella's needs were met…every single one.

The worker turned his radio down and started looking over the area with the generators. Dane stood back and crossed his arms over his chest, calculating and contemplating.

"These are all set to go," Dane assured him. "Aren't you going to the dining area to help?"

The boy shrugged. "Other workers will help out."

Dane stared at the back of the guy's head and clenched his jaw to keep from yelling at the boy for his lazy, entitled attitude. In due time. This jerk had no clue who Dane was or that he'd be fired for that earlier comment as soon as Dane was in charge.

"This is all covered," Dane stated once again. "You and I can both pitch in. This is a nasty storm and every employee here needs to help anywhere they can."

The other guy stood up and turned, his brows drawn in. "I thought Mitch was over maintenance. What's your position?"

Higher than yours, asshole.

"Miss Garcia is waiting on help." Dane gestured toward the doorway. "Let's go."

Dane thought there was going to be an argument, but the guy finally nodded and headed out the door. There was no need to let Stella know about her lazy employee, but Dane wouldn't forget the kid.

By the time they got to the dining area, several employees, all dressed in black, were already bustling around and setting sprigs of evergreen and simple white votives on each of the tables. The lunch decor was quite a bit different than the dinner ambience. For one thing, it was a lot busier. Many couples chose to eat in their room or one of the fantasy rooms during the evening.

There were little changes Dane saw that hadn't been implemented while his mother had been here. The changing of decor being one of them. He liked the touches Stella put on the place—no doubt with her father's permission. The idea of giving the guests a different restaurant feel each time was smart.

The more he saw of Stella—the way she ran this place, the way she actually cared and wasn't just in this for money or recognition—the more he wondered what his mother would've thought of her.

Not that there was any reason to wonder, really. He knew exactly what she'd have thought.

Lara would've loved Stella.

Dane crossed the dining room and cursed himself.

What the hell did he care what his mother would've thought of Stella? The thought was absolutely irrelevant. Stella and her father weren't going to be part of Mirage much longer and Lara would be proud of Dane for getting back what belonged to him.

There she was. Across the room against the two-story windows encased with stone. Stella had on another one of those sexy little dresses that stopped at her knee...this one in red that made her look only more exotic with that dark skin and hair.

Instead of her usual brown boots, she had on black. There were several inches of bare skin between the top of her boot and the hem of her dress. He clenched his fists, aching to touch her.

Soon, he promised himself.

Stella turned to talk to an employee, pointing in the direction of the kitchen, then she nodded and spun back around. He watched for only a minute before she shifted that dark gaze to him. Even from across the room he could read her body language. She was exhausted, but running on pure determination.

She offered him a soft smile and the gesture hit him square in the gut. Out of this crowd of people she focused on him and the unspoken bond that they shared shouldn't have his heart clenching, but damn it...

There was no room for distractions, no matter how tempting and captivating. He wanted her physically, something he hadn't expected. But he could at least control the passion. Desire and sex were easy—as long as he stayed in control, kept himself from getting too attached and kept her away from his ugly scars.

The true problem came from all the other unwanted, unexplained feelings that were flooding in before he had a chance to shut the damn door on his emotions.

Hadn't he locked that once already? How the hell had this woman, in such a short amount of time, managed to kick it down?

Dane made his way across the room, circling the tables and weaving through chairs not quite set in place yet. Once he reached her, Dane used every ounce of his willpower not to reach out and touch her or to pull her out of this room so he could force her to rest.

But resting wasn't Stella's style. They were cut from the same proverbial cloth in that they didn't rest when there was still work to be done.

"All hands on deck, huh?" he asked when she came to stand right before him.

With a smile and a nod, she replied, "Something like that."

"What do you want?"

Stella quirked her brow. "That's a loaded question."

"It was meant to be."

He might not be able to touch her, but that didn't mean he couldn't let her know exactly what he wanted.

"In that case, I wouldn't mind being away from here, somewhere secluded so I could do anything I wanted for just one day." She closed her eyes and sighed before meeting his gaze again. "But since that's not happening anytime soon, maybe you could check in at the front desk and make sure everything is okay?"

Dane nodded. "Not a problem."

When he started to turn, she called his name. "Be in my room at eight."

Already turned on by her demand, Dane leaned toward her to whisper, "You'd better be ready for me."

Her visual tremble had him whistling on his way out. Damn if she wasn't sexy. She'd been all authoritative, but then when he'd turned the tables, she practically melted to a puddle.

Dane had every intention of doing whatever he could to help her make sure this storm went unnoticed by the guests. But tonight, well, Stella would be his and there was no better recipe for seduction than to be snowbound with a sultry vixen.

Eleven

Stella stared at all the food and the special bottle she'd had brought up just for Dane. Was she a complete and utter fool? How could she feel so strongly for a man when she'd only just met him a few days before?

Yet he'd proved time and time again that he was selfless—both in the bedroom and out. He'd jumped at the chance to help her and pitch in around the resort since some employees couldn't make their shifts. He'd helped work in areas she hadn't even asked, putting in hard labor during what was supposed to be his vacation.

Was that why it was nearly quarter after eight and he still hadn't made it to her penthouse? Perhaps he'd fallen into bed like all the other workers she'd put on sleep rotation.

There had been some serious shuffling of cots and blow-up mattresses in order to fit in the staff members who would be resting while others filled in.

She'd already made a mental note to give each employee a bonus for all their hard work. She hadn't heard one complaint and anything she'd asked, they'd gotten right to handling.

Yet now she stood with her thoughts and her concerns. Not over Mirage or the raging storm. Those two were easy to manage. But Dane proved to be a much more unpredictable beast.

Stella padded through her penthouse and went to the fire. There was nothing like coming back here at the end of a long day and staring at the flickering red and gold flames. A glass of wine in her hand never hurt, either, but she was waiting on Dane.

"Stupid," she muttered to herself and turned away from the fire. Even that wasn't calming her nerves.

Dane was likely just as worn down as she was. Maybe he'd even had enough of her. Why was he busting his ass so much anyway? What was he getting out of all of this? Nothing here was his responsibility, his future didn't hinge on how well this resort ran if the power went out and the road didn't open for several days.

Jerking the rubber band from her wrist, Stella pulled her hair atop her head and twisted it into a knot. She should eat something since she'd brought leftovers from the kitchen up to her room. She hadn't had much time for eating earlier, between bustling from common rooms to suites to fantasy rooms and thinking about her night with Dane.

Just as she popped a cube of smoked gouda into her mouth, the buzzer on her private elevator echoed through the penthouse. Nerves curled together in her belly, which was so silly. Dane was just a man and he was a temporary man at that. Their time would likely draw to a close as soon as the road opened and he was on his way. He had already overstayed his time here and his reservation was technically up. Not that she cared or would kick him out at first chance.

Was she an even bigger fool because she felt a little sliver of emptiness at the thought of him leaving?

Honestly, she didn't care that she was getting in over her head. Dane had shown her so much compassion and support during these past couple of days. And the things that man could do in the bedroom? Her body tingled just thinking about his talents. Even if she got to keep him for only a short time, it would be worth it. That man would certainly fuel fantasies for years to come.

The elevator door slid aside and there he was. A man in a bespoke suit couldn't have looked more powerful, more confident and in control. He had that whole rugged rancher look down to a perfectly imperfect manner. The plaid shirt, the worn jeans, the scuffed cowboy boots.

And those eyes. Dark as midnight surrounded by inky lashes any woman would envy.

Dane came toward her, but his eyes scanned the room before landing back on her.

"You worked all day and came back here to set up dinner?" he asked, obviously shocked.

Stella shrugged, not sure how to take his tone. Was he surprised in a good way or a bad way?

"I may not be able to escape to that remote location I dream of, but this is close enough."

She took a step toward him, closing the gap. Stella reached up, flicking his top button until it slid through the hole. She glanced from her fingertips on his shirt up to his coal-like gaze.

"And if you're here, I don't really care where I am," she added. "Maybe for tonight, we can pretend we're just like any other guest and…"

His hand covered hers. "And what?"

Stella laughed and shook her head. "I'm being silly. You *are* a normal guest."

Dane tipped her head up, framing her face with those rough, firm hands. "I'm a guest, but nothing about this stay has been normal."

"No, I guess not." Stella sighed and took a step back. "I probably shouldn't throw myself at a man who just came off an engagement."

The corner of his mouth tipped up. "No, maybe not, but I never asked you to stop."

"You didn't," she agreed. "But before you rip my clothes off—"

"I believe that was you working on my clothes when I'd barely taken a few steps in."

"Details." Stella waved her hand in the air. "Anyway. I have something for you, something other than leftovers from the kitchen."

She turned toward the bar area separating the living room and kitchen. Tucked perfectly on the other side of the domed lids, she pulled out the white bag and presented it to Dane.

He eyed the gift she clutched in her hand, but he didn't take a step to get it.

"You found time to get me something?" he asked. "In the midst of a raging snowstorm and running a resort full of anxious guests with cabin fever?"

"You're not the only one with pull," she stated.

Dane quirked one thick, dark brow and reached for the bag. "You didn't have to get me anything."

"I didn't do it because of the lotions you got me," she told him. "I did it because I wanted to thank you for everything you've done. You didn't have to be so amazing."

"It's a character trait I can't shake."

Stella couldn't help but laugh at his dry humor as he reached into the bag and pulled out the bottle she had procured from a secret stash that only certain employees knew about.

"Stella." He turned the bottle around and stared at it for a long moment before turning his attention back to her. "This is… I've never had anyone give me a gift like this."

Seriously? He'd been engaged, he had a brother, and a bottle of rare bourbon had him struggling to find words? Even her selfish father gave her gifts—granted, the gifts were given only on birthdays and Christmas and always delivered by his assistant or, in the early years, the nanny. But still…

"It's just bourbon," she muttered, suddenly wondering if she'd gone too far. They were just casually involved and she'd had no clue this would be so emotional for him. "I knew we had a couple bottles of important liquor hidden for special guests or clients who had requests."

He continued clutching the bottle. "I didn't request it."

"It's a gift."

Dane stared down at the bottle, the muscle in his jaw ticked as he remained silent. She'd definitely done something wrong because she'd thought he'd be a bit happier.

"If you'd rather another brand, I know we have several bottles of—"

His eyes snapped to hers. "No. This is… This is

more than thanks enough. I'm just surprised since these bottles are hard to come by."

Stella smiled. "Not so difficult."

He raked that dark gaze over her and she knew full well he knew just how powerful that visual caress was.

"I don't need to be paid, or to get lavish gifts," he told her as he set the bottle on the table and closed the distance between them. "I already told you I'm a simple man."

"The way you're looking at me proves how simple you are."

Dane snaked an arm around her waist and hauled her flush against him. Stella flattened her palms against his chest and tipped her head back to meet his hungry gaze.

"You deserve better," he murmured against her lips. "But I can't pull myself away."

Stella threaded her fingers through his coarse hair. "I never asked you to go and I'll decide what I deserve. Right now, I deserve for you to make this ache go away."

Dane's hands slid down the curve of her body, those talented fingers slid beneath the hem of her skirt and teased along the edge of her lacy panties. So close. So, so close. She wanted him, she didn't care about anything else right now. She didn't care about what was happening between them, because she was positive there was more going on here than sex. Though at that moment, sex was all she wanted.

As for the long term, she had her goals and Dane…well, she assumed his were substantial since he'd been so tight-lipped about them.

"I feel a little guilty." She arched into his touch, barely suppressing a moan. "Doing this while everyone is trapped here."

Dane's low chuckle vibrated against her chest. "I assure you, nobody is complaining they're stuck at a couples' resort with fantasy rooms. And they're doing the same thing we are."

"Does that mean I can take a minute off?"

Dane eased back, drew his brows in and gripped her backside. "I assure you, this will take more than a minute."

Stella sure hoped so because she wanted as much of Dane as she could get. She'd never felt more alive, more powerful than when she was with Dane.

The way he held her, looked at her, worshipped her, were all so new, so exhilarating. There was no reason not to just take what she wanted.

Being stranded with a sexy stranger wasn't something that happened every day, right?

Before she could continue her justifications, Dane palmed her backside and lifted her up as he carried her toward the balcony.

"My bedroom is the other way."

Lips trailed down her throat. "I want you out in the open, where I can see everything."

He stepped out onto the glass-enclosed patio. The one-way windows allowed them to see down to the valley below, but nobody could see in. Still, the idea of being exposed was erotic and thrilling. She knew her guests took full advantage of the various hot tubs positioned on the glass balconies, but she'd had no reason to come out here for anything like this before.

Dane eased her to her feet and made quick work of stripping her of her clothes. When she reached for him, she fully expected him to push her away.

And he did, but he grasped her hands in his. Dark eyes held hers and something other than passion looked back at her. There was that heaviness of pain once again. She'd seen that emotion in his eyes before, but never when they'd been on the brink of driving each other out of their minds with want and need.

"I need to tell you something."

His words were coated with a raw, emotional tone she'd never heard from him. Stella turned her hands over beneath his. She might be standing before him completely stripped, but Dane was much more exposed, much more vulnerable.

"I…I have secrets." The muscle in his jaw clenched as he glanced down to their joined hands, then back up to her face. "Before this goes further, you need to know that I never expected this."

"I never expected finding a sexy stranger, either," she countered with a slight smile, hoping to put him at ease. "You don't have to tell me your deepest, darkest secrets. We have no strings."

"I know, but…"

Dane released her hands and stepped back. Stella wished she'd left something on now that she stood there without him so near. But she realized he wasn't staring at her, he was reaching behind his back and gripping his shirt. With a quick jerk, he had it off and then fisted the material in his hands.

"When I was in the army, I lost some buddies." He stared down as he continued to twist his shirt. "There was an accident. Details aren't necessary here, but the scars are—"

"Stop." Stella reached for him and pulled the shirt away. She dropped it to the floor and raked her eyes over his chest. "I don't care about scars and you don't owe me any type of explanation."

The dark hair covering his chest and abdomen, the tattoo curving over his right shoulder…none of that seemed to hide any imperfections that she could see. She ran her hands over him, up his arms to his chest, down toward the top of his jeans.

"You feel fine," she murmured. "You look fine."

Without a word, she moved around to his back. Stella's breath caught in her throat, instant tears burning her eyes. She slid her fingertips over the puckered scars and obvious burns.

"You don't have to—"

"You look and feel fine here, too," she affirmed, not wanting him to offer her an out. She didn't *need* an out. She needed to make him feel that he was worthy of her, that she appreciated the fact he trusted her enough to tell her, show her.

Dane's entire body remained rigid beneath her touch. Ignoring his obvious discomfort, Stella stepped into him, resting her cheek against his back and wrapping her arms around his waist.

"Did you think this would turn me off?" she asked.

"I've never shown anyone," he murmured. "It's not exactly a time I want to talk about."

Stella pressed her lips to his back, then moved on and placed another kiss, then another. "I wasn't in the mood to talk anyway, cowboy."

Her lips traveled all over until she moved to the front and placed them on that ink over his chest and shoulder. Taking his face between her hands, Stella forced him to meet her gaze.

"You're still wearing too many clothes."

He kept that dark, pained gaze locked on her. "You don't deserve this."

Stella threaded her fingers through his hair and pulled his lips to hers. "I know what I want, Dane. Now stop talking."

Dane surprised her by nipping at her lips, then easing back to slide his fingertip down the valley between her breasts. "Have your way with me."

The low, rumbling words filled the space between them and Stella wasted no time in removing those jeans that hugged his lean hips so deliciously.

Dane may be imperfect in his mind, but to her… well, he was the most perfect, stable, comforting aspect of her entire life.

Now she had to figure out what to do when he chose to leave.

Twelve

"Get down!"

Dane fell to his stomach, using his elbows to crawl away from the knoll. The blast shook the ground. The air was filled with the sound of men screaming in pain. And then something hit his back so hard, the air left his lungs.

One second everything was chaos and hell, then it was quiet and hell. His back burned like nothing he'd ever experienced, but he couldn't lose himself in the pain. He needed to get to his buddies. Reese and Bagger were on the other side of their Humvee. If he could crawl to them, they could somehow get out of here.

With each pull he took to move himself forward

with his arms, the pain in his back seemed to inten-
sify. There was something heavy pressing against
him. If he could just get to his buddies, maybe they
could help each other.

But the quiet seemed to grow. Being out in the
open, shouldn't he hear something? Those cries mo-
ments ago had stopped, leaving only his own grunts
as he dragged himself to the front of the vehicle.

Dane looked around the front, fully expecting to
see his comrades, but there was only one person.
Stella. She smiled at him.

"Help me," he cried. "Help."

She squatted down and smirked. "Help you? Like
you helped me lose everything? You're on your own,
Dane. That's how you like it anyway."

"Stella, please." He just needed this weight gone.
He couldn't breathe, and the pain had him fading
fast. "Stella. Stella."

He kept calling for her. Why wasn't she answer-
ing him?

"Stella!"

That weight on his back finally shifted, then some-
thing kept pounding against him. Over and over.
Dane pushed away, tried to pull in a breath, but he
wasn't getting enough oxygen. He was dying and
Stella had walked away.

"Dane."

He jerked up, panting. The frantic tone in Stella's
voice had him blinking against the darkness. With

the sheet pooled around his waist, Dane gripped the edge of the fabric and attempted to regain some normalcy to his breathing.

Her hand went to his back and Dane cringed, still not used to the touch there and not ready to be consoled after the same damn nightmare that had plagued him for years.

No. Not the same. This time the ending was quite different and almost more disturbing than the usual horrendous scene.

He didn't have to be Dr. Freud to understand what the dream meant. In it, she'd obviously found out about his plan. She'd discovered he'd been lying to her, that he'd stolen her business from her.

But it wasn't hers. Not now, not later. Mirage could never belong to her and he shouldn't feel guilt when he wasn't the one who put her in this position.

Yet guilt still gripped him by the throat and made it damn near impossible to breathe.

He jerked the covers aside and rose from the bed. His eyes adjusted easily to the dark; he'd been living in darkness for years so this wasn't new.

"Dane."

That soft voice, the voice that belonged to a woman who cared for him, who saw his scars and wasn't bothered by them.

"I can't stay." He searched for his clothes and didn't look back at her when the sheets rustled.

"I shouldn't have fallen asleep here to begin with. I know what happens."

He scooped up his shirt, but couldn't find his damn pants.

"The nightmares?" she asked. "You weren't dreaming of the war. You were screaming for me to help you. So let me."

Those slender arms came around his chest, pinning him in place before he could put his shirt on. She wanted to help, but if she knew the truth she'd turn away from him, just as she had in the dream.

Dane didn't want to hurt her. Hell, he didn't purposely want to hurt anybody, except for Robert, but he wanted what belonged to him. Why did all the paths leading to his goal get more twists and turns and roadblocks?

"I never stay with a woman," he admitted. "Not since the accident. But you're…different."

"All the more reason for you to quit running." She circled around to the front and gripped his biceps. "I'm here. I'm not asking you to leave, I'm not asking you to talk about anything if you don't want to. But I am asking you to give me a chance. Don't shut me out."

Give her a chance? That's not what he'd come here for, but damn it. He couldn't help himself and now anything they had was based on a foundation of deception.

"I wasn't lying when I said you don't deserve this."

He fisted his shirt and wished like hell he'd found some other way to get what he wanted. "I won't be here long and you're dealing with your father—"

Stella's soft laugh filled the room, her warm breath tickled his bare chest. "You know how to ruin a mood. Yes, I'm dealing with my father, but right now, I'm dealing with you."

"I'll go back to my room," he offered. "It's best that way."

"Best? For you?" she asked. "Because the best thing for me is for you to stay. You obviously trusted me enough to show me your scars. Let me see the ones you're hiding on the inside."

There was nothing else he wanted more than to let her in completely. But they were at odds with each other, though she had no idea who he truly was. This seduction had gotten out of hand, his guilt had grown more and more, and damn it, he actually cared about her.

There was no way he could prevent her from being hurt. None. Even if he walked away and gave up on Mirage—which he could never do—she'd still be hurt by her father's callous treatment and failure to keep his bargains. All he could do at this point was either keep going and enjoy this time with her while it lasted, or start to put some distance between them. She would hate him in the end anyway. Did it matter when that started?

"You can't want more," he warned. "I'm leaving when the mountain clears."

Stella's hands fell away. "I know you are. I guess I was just hoping you would stay a little extra time."

If only she knew the irony in her statement.

"I don't want to get too deep," he added. "There's so much we both have going on and this fling…"

"Doesn't have to end."

She reached for the shirt he held on to and dropped it onto the floor. Taking him by the hand, Stella led him toward the bed. He was utterly defenseless. He was also a bastard. Going back to his room was the smart move, but clearly he'd not been making smart decisions since coming to Mirage because now he had a sinking feeling Stella was falling for him.

As she lay next to him, with her arm over his chest and leg over his thighs like she dared him to leave again, all Dane could think of was that he'd been too busy enjoying her to pull out the secrets he'd come here to discover.

Darkness transitioned into light and Dane continued to stare up at the ceiling. Stella had fallen asleep, but now she stirred. He'd been lying here too long with his thoughts, with his damn guilt that gnawed a hole in his gut.

How was lying to this innocent woman honoring his mother? That's not the type of person Lara Anderson had been. She'd been kind and caring and so giving and loyal. She'd been perfect and Dane, well, he was anything but.

"I want to buy Mirage."

The words were out before he could talk himself out of admitting the truth—or at least a partial truth.

Stella's hand pressed against his chest as she lifted slightly to look down at him. Her hair flattened against one side of her head where she'd slept against his side, her heavy lids shielded half her eyes.

"What?"

Dane swallowed and tucked one arm behind his head. "I want to buy Mirage."

"Yeah, I heard you." She shook her head as she sat all the way up and shifted to face him. "But it's not for sale."

"Everything is for sale for the right price."

She stared back at him as if seeing him for the first time—as if she was finally seeing the man beneath the facade. But she still didn't know the truth.

"My father is turning this over to me," she told him as she let out a laugh. "And I'm certainly not selling it."

Dane remained still. "Are you *certain* your father is going to give this place to you?"

A flash of irritation followed by determination crossed her face. Stella tipped her chin and shoved her hair away from her face. "I won't settle for anything less. I know I'm not what he envisioned for this business or any business of his, really. A son would've already had his choice of companies. I ask for one and I'm jumping through damn hoops to secure it."

So her father's issue was that his only child was a girl? What the hell kind of backward thinking was that?

Dane clenched his teeth and eased up onto one elbow. "Your father won't be the one keeping this resort," he vowed.

Stella's brows drew in. "I'm not following you this morning. You didn't get any sleep, did you?"

He reached for her hand and gave it a reassuring squeeze. "This has nothing to do with last night."

A total lie. This had *everything* to do with last night. He'd let her in, deeper than he'd let anyone. He'd seen a side of her he hadn't expected and damn it, he respected her.

None of this was going according to plan and now he was just winging everything and he hoped like hell his goals didn't vanish forever now that they were finally within reach.

"Your father will not be the owner of Mirage for much longer," Dane reiterated. "I promise."

"I still don't get it," she muttered. "Do you know something I don't? And if you say you know my father, that you actually do work for him, I will throw you out into that blizzard—"

"No. I don't know him." Not personally anyway. "And I certainly don't work for him. But I've dealt with men like him before. He won't hold on to this place and he won't turn it over to you because all he cares about is money."

If he cared half as much about his daughter, that would be a nice step in the right direction.

Dane didn't want to ask more questions, didn't want to get more involved emotionally than he already was. But he couldn't stop himself.

"Were you two always at odds?" he asked. "When you were growing up, what was he like?"

Stella shrugged and took her fingertip to the back of his hand. She drew imaginary circles around his knuckles as she seemed to be contemplating her words.

"He wasn't around much. My mom died when I was born, so he hired a nanny." She chewed on her bottom lip as she went around another knuckle. "When he was there, I was never good enough at anything I tried. I loved skiing and would take my thoughts out to the slopes. One lesson turned into another and years later I found myself competing at national levels."

Dane knew that was the extremely shortened version because anyone who competed at that level had worked their ass off for years, giving up most of their social life for the ultimate goal.

"I think he blames me for her death," she went on, emotion lacing her tone. "He's never come right out and said so, but he's hinted enough."

"It wasn't your fault. You know that, right?"

Stella remained silent as she glanced away.

"You're not responsible for her death," he stressed as he sat all the way up. "Listen to me."

Dane took her bare shoulders and turned her to face him before he framed her face and forced her to hold his gaze.

"Whatever you grew up believing, whatever he said or just implied, you know nothing was your fault."

Stella stared back and shrugged. "It was not exactly my fault, but if I hadn't been born maybe she and my dad would still be married. Maybe they would've had other children. Boys—to fulfill all the requirements to be a Garcia heir."

Dane couldn't wait to take this resort back and get Stella out from under her father's ruling thumb. She might hate Dane in the end, but at least she'd be saved from one bastard.

"You don't really believe that." Dane wanted to shake sense into her, but he'd only known her a handful of days and he couldn't exactly reprogram her from over twenty years of dealing with her father. "You're stronger than your father. You wouldn't be here if you were weak. Being a woman is actually your strength. Women think in a different way than men and this resort needs you."

Stella attempted a smile. "Nobody has ever acted

like I'm needed here or at any other business, for that matter."

"Then everyone is a damn fool."

He meant every word. She was valuable, and she'd done wonderful work here. The only problem was that he just couldn't have her take his resort.

"You're a sharp businesswoman and if your dad can't see that, then stop beating yourself up and go out and make something of your own without worrying about how he'd react."

"That's easy for you to say," she retorted. "I don't have unlimited means of income. Everything I have is from my salary, but it's not a lot. My father considers room and board enough. This resort, this little piece of his life is all I've ever wanted. I gave up on his love a long time ago, but getting his respect is something I may never give up wanting."

"Why?"

"Because he only deals in business," she explained. "Respect for my business abilities may be the closest thing to love that he can give. I don't know that he's capable of love in the way that I need it."

Not likely, but since Dane didn't know how to love anyone like they needed, he wasn't the person to offer advice on this matter.

His cell rang, breaking the tension and giving him the out he needed.

"I need to take that," Dane explained as he eased off the bed.

He scooped up his jeans and pulled the cell from his pocket. With a quick glance to the screen, he saw it was Ethan.

"I'm just going to step out here." He started for the patio when her words stopped him.

"That's not your ex-fiancée wanting you back, is it?"

Ex-fiancée. Damn it. Dane had gotten so swept away in this whole charade, he'd forgotten about the fictitious woman.

"I promise, it's nobody wanting me back."

Possessive girlfriends had never been an issue in his life because no one had ever been allowed to get that close. He was fine with that. There was no need to chance having your heart ripped out again. Once was more than enough for him when he lost his mother. The ranch kept him busy and that was all he needed. Well, that and Mirage.

Dane swiped the screen and glanced over his shoulder to see Stella sliding beneath the covers, her hand going to the dent in his pillow.

Swallowing the guilt, he answered. "It's awfully early for you, isn't it?"

"I haven't been to bed, yet," Ethan replied. "I figured being a rancher you're always up at this time anyway."

"I'm not on the ranch."

"I'm aware," Ethan growled. "Shut up and listen. Robert is due to be at Sunset Cove in three days."

Dane gripped his cell. "How do you know? And are you positive?"

"My sources confirmed his travel arrangements. How soon can you get here?"

"You're already there?" Dane shook his head and glanced to the hot tub where hours ago he'd pleasured Stella until she cried out his name.

The memories of her would last him a lifetime, which was good since she'd hate him in the very near future.

"I'm here," Ethan confirmed.

"Just make sure you keep the goal in mind—and I don't mean bikini-clad women."

His brother chuckled. "No reason I can't enjoy myself while I wait."

There was static on the line and Ethan's muffled voice a moment before he said, "I'll text you updates. I gotta go."

The call ended, leaving Dane wondering just how quick he could wrap things up here. Ruiz needed to be dealt with here and now. The next number Dane would have his broker throw out would be impossible to turn down. Maybe he could make things move faster by appealing to Ruiz's male chauvinist side.

Dane stared out the window as the sun started peeking over the mountaintops. The snow had stopped sometime during the night, which was good news for the stranded guests.

With another quick glance over his shoulder,

Dane sent a text to his broker with the new offer and stipulations. There was no way this would be turned down. Ruiz was a smart businessman. If all went as planned, this resort would be his in thirty days.

Thirteen

Stella had never taken advantage of a fantasy suite. She had her own penthouse for one thing, but the main reason was she'd never had a need or a man.

Well, now she had both.

Butterflies fluttered in her stomach and she had no clue why she was nervous. It wasn't like she was a virgin or hadn't slept with Dane before. Over the past several days, they'd been all over each other.

The blizzard had calmed down to Montana's usual snow accumulation and guests came and went, still cautious of slippery roads. All was mostly back to normal.

Except Dane stayed. His stay was technically up

two days ago and his penthouse had been taken by a couple celebrating their tenth wedding anniversary.

So she moved his stuff into her suite.

Stella jerked on the tie of her shirt. She couldn't believe she had donned this outfit, but she figured Dane would like it. At least, she hoped he went for that whole lumberjack girl vibe. She'd taken one of her plaid flannels and left all buttons undone, simply tying the bottom in a knot just below her breasts. She figured the bright red lacy bra beneath was a nice touch.

Then she'd found an old denim skirt and ended up taking a pair of scissors to it to make it about four inches shorter. Dane would love the present beneath the skirt.

Of course she couldn't exactly parade through her resort looking like she was about to take the stage as a strip club's version of *Twin Peaks* with her boobs on display. That wouldn't be professional at all and her father's minion, whoever that might be, would certainly be all too eager to tattle.

Stella had put a fake name into the computer system to block off the room for the night and she'd sneaked in with her costume in her purse. She still wore her knee boots, but she had pulled her hair from the twist and left it in a wild mess around her shoulders.

She pulled her cell from her back pocket and checked the time. Dane should be here any minute. She'd told him she needed help moving something in the Lumberjack Room and he'd said he'd be right there.

Now she waited.

Stella crossed the hardwood floor and put the cell in her bag in the corner. A click of the door had her spinning back around.

Dane stepped through the door, took in the lanterns all around the room, the hanging tent, and the bourbon bar.

Then his eyes scanned back to her. The dark gaze raked over her, up and down. Then another slow, visual perusal.

"So I'm assuming you don't want to move anything," he said as he reached behind him, flicking the lock into place.

He crossed to the middle of the room and put his hand on the small wooden steps leading to the tent. He peered inside and back to her.

"This thing hold people?" he asked.

Stella smiled. "It's secure for up to eight hundred pounds."

Dane hooked his thumbs through his belt loops as his gaze took another travel down her body. "Then I guess we're safe."

Safe? She was anything but safe with him. At least not emotionally because she was pretty sure she was falling for him, which was ridiculous considering she'd known him just over a week. The level of feelings she *thought* she had couldn't be developed in such a short time...could it?

"Something is rolling around inside that head of yours," he stated, pulling her from her thoughts. "Maybe you need a distraction."

"Oh, believe me. You've distracted me since you got here."

Dane kept that dark gaze on hers as his mouth kicked up in a grin and he pulled on his belt buckle. "That's the nicest compliment I've ever received."

"You *would* take that as a compliment."

Dane stood before her with his jeans unfastened, belt dangling, and reached for the hem of his shirt. "Why did you go to this trouble? We could've just stayed in your penthouse."

Stella shrugged. "I wanted to change it up a little. I never know when you're going to leave, so I guess I wanted to—"

"Give me a going away present?" he asked.

When he whipped his shirt over his head, she felt a warm glow of satisfaction at the realization that he'd gotten so comfortable with being bare around her he no longer even hesitated to take off his shirt. Everything about being together had become natural and effortless. They'd fallen into an easy pattern of making love at night, and when she worked during the day he would text to check on her or he'd make himself scarce and let her work. He never tried to tell her how to do her job and he'd never mentioned buying Mirage again and she certainly hadn't brought it up.

"Let's not talk about you leaving," she added. "I'd rather focus on you and this fantasy of mine."

Dane quirked a brow. "Did you have any man in mind for this fantasy?"

She took a step toward him and toyed with the tie between her breasts. "I didn't even think of this fantasy until I saw you."

He reached out, easing her hands aside, and slid apart the knot holding her shirt closed. Dane's fingertips grazed over her skin as he pushed the material from her shoulders. Stella shrugged until the shirt fell to the floor.

"I do like this outfit you came up with." He caressed the line on her skin just above the lacy edge of her bra. "I don't think I've seen you wear this around the resort before. Is this special for me?"

"You know it is."

His hand slid down and he curled his fingers inside her waistband, tugging her toward him. "I like knowing you thought of me, of this. Nobody has ever done anything like this before."

Which would explain the lack of fiancée now.

"First the bourbon and now the fantasy room." Stella smiled. "This has been quite the week for you."

"You have no idea," he murmured. "But let's get to this fantasy."

"Well, as much as I'd love to escape to the middle

of nowhere and just chill, that's not possible for me now. So, I thought I'd bring you here and we could at least pretend to be somewhere else."

Dane unfastened her skirt and sent it down her legs. She kicked it aside, leaving her in her matching red bra and thong set, and her boots.

"I don't care where I am if that's what you're wearing." Dane finished undressing and wrapped an arm around her waist. "Tell me you've never brought another man in here."

Stella rolled her eyes. "What do you think?"

He dipped his head and feathered his lips over the swell of her breasts. "I think I'm damn lucky and I'm done talking."

She fisted his hair and arched her back as he jerked her bra cups aside and feasted on her. His hands gripped her backside as he lifted her off the ground. She wrapped her legs around his waist and let him take total control.

Dane spun toward the suspended, oversize tent and sat her on the open edge. When he eased back, Stella nearly whimpered. But he didn't go far. He reached down to her boots and slid one, then the other off, letting them thunk to the floor.

Stella spread her legs, making room for him. He stepped up onto the bottom rung of the small ladder and curled his fingers around her waist.

"I want to see and taste every damn inch of you,"

he told her as he scooted her back into the pile of pillows. "I'll ruin you for another man."

Stella stilled, her eyes darting to his. Ruin her for another man? What was he saying? Did that mean he wanted more? That he wanted to stay and see what happened?

Little did he know, he'd already ruined her for anybody else. There would never be another man like Dane.

But that was something they'd have to discuss later when he wasn't making her toes curl with passionate promises.

Dane trailed his lips over her chest and down to her abdomen. "You're so damn sexy."

He made her feel that way. She never would've taken another man to the fantasy suite. Sex with Dane was, well, indescribable. She wanted to experience everything with him.

Hooking his thumbs in the silky material of her panties across her hips, he didn't tear them off or jerk them down. Instead he drove her out of her mind with sliding those rough, calloused hands over her heated skin as he slowly eased the material down her legs.

His mouth seemed poised to follow the path of his hands and Stella couldn't control her restlessness. She ached, she needed, she craved.

When he held her knees apart with the width of his broad shoulders, Stella couldn't suppress the

groan that escaped her. And then his mouth was on
her. Those big, firm hands gripped her inner thighs
as he pleasured her in a way she'd never known before.

Stella threaded her fingers through his hair and
arched her back. Dane's relentless urge to please her
had her body spiraling out of control and she didn't
even try to hold back her cries.

The climax hit her so fiercely, Stella shook against
him for what felt like hours until her tremors began
to slow. Before she could fully recover, he was putting on a condom and climbing up to her.

"I'm not nearly done with you."

He gripped the backs of her thighs and slid into
her in one slow, delicious thrust. Then he flipped
them so she straddled him and he smiled up at her.

"Do what you want, cowgirl."

Why did he have to be so sexy? Was there anything about him that didn't turn her on? The relin-
quishing of power right when her body still zinged
and tingled made her feel dizzy and overwhelmed.
She wasn't sure she could even move right now.

Dane playfully smacked her hip. "I'm waiting."

Bracing her hands on his chest, Stella smiled as
she started to move. Dane's fingertips dug into her
thighs as she rocked against him. From the way his
jaw was set, his nostrils flared, and his lids lowered,
she'd guess she was doing just fine.

As she quickened her rhythm, her body started

climbing again. The pleasure became too intense and she leaned down, capturing his mouth with hers.

Dane palmed her backside and urged her faster while he made love to her mouth. He seemed to touch her everywhere all at once, causing that familiar tingling to build and grow until she exploded all around him.

He tightened his hold as he stilled beneath her. His lips moved over hers almost as if he couldn't get enough.

Yeah, he'd definitely ruined her for any other man.

Stella waited until they both stopped trembling before she sat back up and smiled. "Well, I should book this room more often."

Dane reached up and cupped her breasts. "You'll only be booking it with me."

When he said things like that, she couldn't help but think…

"What do you say we take that bottle of bourbon and go upstairs?" he suggested. "I have a few more things I want to do to you."

Mercy. Was he serious? She wasn't sure she could walk on these shaky legs, let alone head in for round two…or three in her case.

Within minutes, though, they were dressed and heading the private back way toward the elevator exclusively for her.

Dane laced his fingers through hers and Stella couldn't help but smile. She hadn't held hands with

a man in, well, years. There was something so innocent, yet so...was *bonding* the right word? After all
they'd done together, the fact he led her back to her
suite by her hand was so damn adorable.

There was no denying she'd fallen in love with
him. What would he do if she actually came out
and told him? Would he vanish? Would he tell her
he felt the same?

Part of her wanted to be completely honest and
open with her feelings. The rest of her wanted to
keep her feelings locked away inside her heart where
they couldn't be hurt or crushed. She'd never told
someone she loved them before.

Maybe she couldn't trust her feelings. What did
she know about love? She'd never known her mother,
her father was about as loving as a tree stump, and
the only other time she'd thought she was in love,
the man had been a cheating scumbag who had been
using her only to impress her father.

Maybe all this amazing sex had her emotions and
thoughts too scattered.

"You're awfully quiet," Dane stated as he punched
the code in to take them up to her penthouse. "Maybe
I wore you out."

Stella squeezed his hand and rested her head on
his shoulder. "I'm not even going to deny that because it's true."

He kissed her forehead. "I'll let you sleep a few
hours before I take you again."

Her body stirred. Just those simple words had her imagining them together again. Each time was just as thrilling as the first. She was half-dressed, and they were entirely alone, so he could have her right here and now and nobody would ever know.

But she really needed to figure out what she was going to do about her feelings…how to tell him.

Maybe she should actually put some clothes on to have the talk because it didn't seem appropriate to have a serious conversation when her underwear was gone, her shirt was tied over her bare breasts and her skirt was so short her nether regions were nearly showing.

The elevator door slid open and Stella took in everything all at once. The roaring fire that she hadn't started, the overwhelming scent of a pipe and the robust man wearing a suit at nearly midnight.

"Dad. What are you doing here?"

Fourteen

Dane released Stella's hand and stared at the man across the room. So this was Ruiz Garcia. The businessman was clearly all business. Who the hell stayed dressed up at this time of the night?

"I told you I was coming."

Ruiz turned to face them and his eyes widened at the sight of Stella's outfit. "I don't have to ask what you've been doing. Is this typical behavior at my resort for you?"

"Dad, I just—"

"Decided to take advantage of a fantasy suite," Dane chimed in, earning him a glare from Stella. "She's been working her ass off," Dane went on, ignoring her wide eyes. He stepped around her, mostly to shield her half-naked body, but also to shield her from the proverbial big, bad wolf. "This is an adult resort, and it's beautifully managed and maintained, with everything a couple could want. No reason she can't take advantage of the amenities."

Ruiz narrowed his eyes as he slid aside his suit jacket and slid his hands into his pockets. "And you are?"

"He's with me," Stella answered before Dane could.

Ruiz wouldn't recognize Dane's name because each deal that Dane had his broker send had been listed under a business name. Ruiz had no clue who he was really dealing with. But Dane knew exactly what he was up against, which gave him just another edge he needed.

Stella came to stand beside Dane as she crossed her arms over her chest. "You told me the other day that you were coming in a couple weeks. Why are you here now?"

"I had news I wanted to deliver and didn't want to discuss over the phone." Ruiz glanced to Dane. "Perhaps your friend could give us some privacy and you could put some decent clothes on."

Stella stepped forward and Dane remained rooted in place. This was her fight, but he wanted her to know he had her back. If her father started mansplaining or talking like he had the impression he

148

was above her, she could know Dane was there and was totally on her side.

"Dane is staying here with me, so say whatever you need to say."

Ruiz's brow quirked as he glanced between the two. "Well, whatever you have going on is irrelevant to the news I need to pass on. I'm selling Mirage."

Stella gasped. "Does that mean you're giving me the chance to—"

"No." Ruiz pulled in a deep breath and took a step toward his daughter. "I received an offer just today and I'm accepting it. The terms were too good to pass up."

Dane didn't know what to feel, how to react. Clearly he couldn't show any sign of knowing about the offer, even though he had no doubt the offer Ruiz spoke of was his.

After all this time, Mirage would be his. Dane swallowed the lump of emotions at the thought of getting his mother's place back where it belonged.

But he glanced at Stella and all of his elation simply vanished. The look on her face, one of betrayal and pain, sliced right through him.

"You—you're just selling this when you've known how much I want to have it?" she asked.

"Business is business," Ruiz stated with a shrug as if that summed up crushing his daughter's entire world. "If you didn't get so emotionally involved, you would know that and you'd already have a plan B instead of investing your entire future here."

"Plan B?" Stella asked, her voice cracking, revealing just how close to the edge she was. "You're my family—I shouldn't need a plan B for how to prove myself worthy of your time or attention. My entire life I've wanted you to notice me, to make a point to acknowledge that I'm your daughter. Your employees and stockholders rank higher on your priority list than I do."

Ruiz's eyes darted to Dane. "You care to give us a minute?"

"Yeah, actually I do care."

Dane folded his arms over his chest and glared back at the man who was used to people jumping at his every command. The muscle in Ruiz's jaw clenched. Clearly he hadn't expected Dane's response.

"Just tell me why?" Stella demanded. "Why would you do this? Why even give me hope when you planned on selling?"

Ruiz focused his attention back to his daughter and Dane took a step toward her. She stood there not caring about her precarious state of dress as she fought for her future…a future he had stolen from her.

Seeing her pain firsthand was sure as hell nothing he'd planned on. He'd thought he'd be gone before the ramifications of his actions kicked in…and back when he'd made the plan, he honestly hadn't cared enough to even consider how someone else might feel at that moment in time.

Her pain, her obvious anger, couldn't deter him. He still had a goal, he still had to get his mother's resort back where it belonged, and once he had that… well, then he could deal with Stella without her father prying into their business.

Because now Stella was his business. He didn't want her hurt, so all he could do at this point was try to make things less crushing. He had no idea how, but he'd damn well figure out something for her because unlike her bastard father, Dane actually cared about Stella's future.

"What was the offer?" Stella asked.

More than you have, sweetheart.

Yet Mirage was all he'd ever wanted. Money was just paper, not what kept him driven. Revenge and justice kept him pushing forward each and every day of his life.

"The offer was well over what I paid for this resort, so the profit will be a nice chunk in my pocket," Ruiz replied with a smug smile. "I'm sure we can find something else for you to do."

"I don't want anything else," Stella growled. "You know this is what I wanted. I love the story behind it, I love the setting, the idea. I love every aspect. Do you even know that kind of passion?"

Ruiz narrowed his gaze at his daughter. "Don't

preach to me about passion. It's my passion that gave you any opportunity you ever had. Money is the greatest passion of all."

"That's sad if that's truly how you feel," Stella told him.

Dane pressed a hand to the small of her back. Of course Ruiz would hang his black heart on his finances. He probably slept with a bag of money as a security blanket.

"I never cared about money growing up," Stella cried. "I wanted you there. I'd lost my mother and I never really had a father."

"You had opportunities most kids dream of," Ruiz spat back. "So maybe you should be thanking me instead of whining. Without me, you would've been in the foster system and then what would've happened?"

Stella gasped. "Foster care? What are you talking about?"

Ruiz sneered and dread curled through Dane.

"Your mother had an affair. I'm not your father."

Stella reached out for something stationary to hold on to, to help her remain standing. But her knees shook, buckled, and only Dane's strong, familiar arms wrapping around her kept her from collapsing.

She leaned back against him as she stared at her father.

No. Not her father. A man who wanted accolades

for his half-hearted efforts in keeping her out of the system.

"You're lying," she accused, not really knowing what else to say. Dane's strength kept her up, but she held on to his forearm for fear he'd let her go.

"I'm not," her father said. "She cheated on me and her lover was your father."

How could he just now be dropping this bomb on her? Why after all of these years did he want to purposely continue hurting her?

"I want his name." She straightened her shoulders and stood straight up, but didn't let go of Dane. "I want to know who my real father is."

"He's dead."

Stella stared at him for a moment before she let out a laugh. "You're such a liar. You're going to great lengths to ensure I hate you forever."

"Fine, if you need to know, then his name was Martin Hernandez. He was killed in a small commuter plane crash when you were two. Look him up if you don't believe me. Use my investigator. I had a paternity test done to prove in case I needed it for future reference, but he died before—"

"What? Before you could blackmail him or hold me over his head?" Stella snarled. "Why did you even keep me? Why not just give me to him when I was born?"

"Because he hit your mother when she told him about the pregnancy." Ruiz might have had a flash of remorse in his eyes if he had a heart. "I might be a bastard, but I don't condone hitting a woman. Besides, I grew up in the foster system and I didn't want that for Maggie's baby."

Stella fisted her hands at her sides and had no clue what to do next. How did anyone react when their entire world was ripped away? First her mother passed, then her father—who wasn't her father—kept her out of some semblance of pity, only to pawn her off on nannies and teachers and coaches. And now? Well, now that she thought she could get somewhere with her life, somewhere that might make her father take notice and maybe see her as a worthy businesswoman, that opportunity was stripped away.

As much as she wanted to scream and shed tears, Stella wouldn't dare show Ruiz any emotion. He didn't deserve to know that he could affect her. All of these years and she'd never gotten anything from him by way of feelings. That's all she'd wanted, but apparently because she hadn't been his by blood, she hadn't deserved even the slightest hint of true affection.

"I want you to leave."

The words slipped through her lips before she realized she was even thinking them. But as soon as they came out, she realized she really did want him gone. Stella didn't want to look at that smug smirk another second.

"Listen to me," he started, taking a step toward

her. "I didn't purposely set out to hurt you, but things fell into place, both in the past and now. It's out of my hands."

Stella gritted her teeth and used up every ounce of energy not to haul off and hit him. If he wanted her to truly hate him, he needn't say another word.

"All of this was in your hands," she fired back. "You could've told me about my father, you could've told me you had no intention of ever letting me take over this resort. You spied on me because you didn't think I could handle running this place, and then you went behind my back to sell to the highest bidder. Don't act like you couldn't have done anything about this. You've manipulated my life from the start without a moment of care or concern for me. You never had time for me—well, now I have no more time for you. So get the hell out."

Ruiz smoothed his suit jacket down and cleared his throat. "Actually, this resort belongs to me until the new owners take over. So if anyone is leaving it's you. But, since I'm kind enough, I'll give you two weeks to move your things."

Stella glanced around her space. She'd already gotten so used to being here, in this space she called her own.

Swallowing the lump of pain and remorse, Stella focused her attention back on Ruiz. "Who bought Mirage?"

"My assistant handled most of the details, but

I was told Strong L Ranch is going to be the new owner."

Stella chewed on her lip to keep it from quivering. Whoever bought this place couldn't love it near as much as she did. There was no way they had the emotional connection she did. Stella had wanted this place for years and had been so close. So damn close.

"Stella asked you to leave."

Dane's low, commanding tone reminded her he was still here, still supporting her. He'd been quiet, letting her handle things, but she was damn near to the point of breaking. She wanted her father—no, Ruiz—gone. She *needed* him gone.

"I hate that things came to this," Ruiz stated. "You've actually surprised me with your determination and work ethic. I'm sure there's another business that I can—"

"I don't want your businesses and I don't want your pity." Stella pulled in a deep, shaky breath. "I'm done waiting for approval from you. I'm done hoping you'll see me for the woman I am. I'm not a failure, I kick ass at what I do and someone will see that... even if the man who supposedly raised me can't."

Stella turned and crossed to the elevator. She punched the button with more force than necessary, but she had nowhere else to channel all of this anger.

Ruiz stepped into the elevator and Stella forced herself to look at him. She wanted him to see that she wasn't weak, no matter how many times he had continued to knock her down. He may have shown a sliver of nobility by raising another man's kid, but Stella knew he regretted every day he'd been stuck with her. She'd never truly been his daughter, and as much as that hurt, she was glad she knew the truth.

He continued to hold her stare as the doors slid closed.

And then he was gone.

All the energy, all the emotions from the last hour took their toll. Stella flattened her hand over the elevator keypad and dropped her head. Tears burned her eyes, every word she didn't know to say got caught in her throat.

Strong arms wrapped around her. Dane eased her around until she faced him, then he scooped her up without a word. Stella looped her arms around his neck and shut her eyes as he carried her away. As strong as she prided herself on being, there were times she just couldn't hold it together anymore. Everyone had a breaking point and Stella had more than reached hers.

Dane set her on her feet and Stella blinked up at him. He'd carried her to the bed and he started undressing her.

"I don't have the—"

Dane placed his finger over her lips, cutting off her words. "You're going to rest. That's all you need to do right now. Nothing can be done about the resort or Ruiz right this minute. Just let me care for you."

Tears continued to slide down her cheeks. Stella swatted at them. "I'm not weak," she defended.

Dane framed her face with his hands and forced her attention on him. "Baby, I never thought you were. You just got the wind knocked out of you. I'm here and I'm not going anywhere."

Stella lifted one foot, then the other for him to remove her boots. When he straightened back up, Stella rested her head against his chest and inhaled that masculine, woodsy scent she'd come to associate with Dane.

"Why haven't you left yet?" she muttered.

She thought he murmured something about "not being done" but she wasn't sure and she was too tired to ask him to repeat it. All that mattered was that he was there and she knew he would stay for as long as she needed.

Fifteen

"I'll wrap up a few things and then be right there," Dane explained. "I've verbally secured the deal. I need to get back to the ranch and finalize the sale, then I'll pack a bag."

Ethan gripped the cell as he stood on the balcony of his penthouse resort room, overlooking the ocean. He glanced over his shoulder to the owner of the red bikini he'd met on the beach. She'd been in his bed since.

Harper. Her name was Harper and she had been filling his time and keeping him relaxed while he waited on Robert to get to the island. He hadn't planned on finding the distraction, but there was no way in hell he was turning her down.

"Leave the flannels at home," Ethan replied, turning his attention back to the view of the beach. "Do you even own swim trunks?"

"I'm not coming to work on my tan," Dane growled. "We're halfway to our goal. Do you think you can stay focused?"

Memories of the past few days and the curvy woman in his bed flashed through his mind in vivid detail.

"Oh, I'm focused."

Dane let out a sigh. "I'm going to the ranch later today. I'll text you when I'm on my way to Sunset Cove."

Something in his brother's tone had Ethan turning back to make sure the patio door was closed. He crossed the balcony and took a seat on the club chair.

"You don't sound near as thrilled as I thought you'd be."

"I finally have Mirage," Dane muttered. "What more could I want?"

"I don't know. That's why I'm asking."

The line went silent and Ethan waited. He stared out at the horizon as the sun started creeping up. A new day, and another step closer to finalizing their goals.

So why was Dane so…monotone?

"It's the manager, isn't it?" Ethan guessed. "Is there something going on there?"

"Don't worry about me."

Ethan clenched his teeth, but ultimately decided he was done being pushed aside.

"I've worried about you every single day since Mom died," he stated. "You might have dealt with grief your own way, but I needed you. Damn it. Don't push me out now."

More silence and Ethan wondered if he'd gone too far, revealed too much. He was human and sometimes those emotions just came out. He wasn't sorry he'd finally said something, but he was sorry that this conversation was over the phone.

"I'm not pushing you out," Dane finally said. "Not on purpose anyway. I'm just… Let me get things wrapped up here. This isn't all about the resorts. It's about us."

For the first time in nearly two decades, Ethan had a blossom of hope that he and Dane could get back to where they'd been before their world got ripped to shreds.

"I've got a room booked for you," Ethan assured him. "See you soon. And, Dane? Great job getting your resort. Mom would be proud."

The line went dead.

Ethan stared at his phone before dropping it to his lap and raising his gaze to the sky. Maybe he and Dane had further to go in repairing their relationship than he'd thought. Perhaps the mention of their mother triggered something in Dane.

Ethan didn't know. What he did know was that

there was a vivacious woman in his bed, more than eager to continue this fling for as long as she was in town, and he was *this close* to securing his future and his legacy…and claiming revenge on Robert Anderson.

Dane had packed his meager bag, touched base with his broker and was all set to head back to his ranch.

But he didn't want to leave Mirage. He'd just acquired it—technically. All that was left was to sign the papers, but this was a done deal.

He wasn't frustrated and cranky because he was leaving Stella. No, they'd decided at the beginning this connection or whatever they had would be temporary. Just because he was leaving her while she happened to be already emotionally crushed and shattered because of Ruiz, well…

Damn it.

Dane ran a hand over his stubbled jaw and glanced around the penthouse. His eyes landed on the note he'd left for Stella. She was working and he didn't want to interrupt. Even though she had been dismissed by her father, she was downstairs right now making sure each and every guest had what they needed to ensure a getaway they'd never forget.

And Dane was a damn coward for sneaking out without saying goodbye. He could freely admit it, but there was no way in hell he could stay any longer.

He'd gotten what he came for and hanging around would only prolong the inevitable. Stella needed to move on, and so did he.

So why was there so much pain? Why did that heaviness on his chest leave him feeling like a complete jerk?

Because he was. At this point, Dane was no better than the man who'd raised her. They'd both lied to her, deceived her, betrayed her.

She was still dealing with learning the truth about Ruiz. He couldn't unload more secrets on her. Leaving was the best option—for both of them.

Keep telling yourself that, buddy. Maybe you'll believe the lies.

Gripping the handle of his suitcase, Dane headed toward the elevator. He'd be back. This would be his suite when he returned, but he knew in his heart things wouldn't be the same.

When he'd first arrived he could see only one woman here—his mother. Now he knew when he returned, he'd see only Stella.

She'd left an imprint on his life and on this place that would never disappear. There was something so permanent about her. They'd forged a bond whether he wanted to admit it or not.

And he didn't want to admit any such thing.

Since he knew the layout of this place better than his own home, Dane slipped out in such a way that he knew Stella would never see him. He could be honest enough with himself to admit that if he saw her and attempted to explain why he was leaving, the guilt would consume him.

Dane had to push that aside. He couldn't allow anything to steal the moment he'd been preparing for. Once this was all officially his, he'd feel better. All he had to do was finalize the sale, and get to Ethan. Working with his brother to bring down Robert would only add to the euphoria of finally reclaiming everything they'd been robbed of.

Once they came in contact with Robert, well, there would be a little surprise waiting for him. Their miserable bastard of a stepfather was done stealing and being deceitful. He wouldn't be free to ruin anybody else's lives or rob futures.

Dane started to head toward the back hallway from another hallway he'd sneaked through, but a familiar voice through the door leading to the back office stopped him.

"Come to me for any specialty needs for the fantasy rooms," Stella stated.

"What about Savannah?" an unfamiliar voice asked.

"Her daughter has her first dance recital tonight and tomorrow. I told her to take the days off. Family is too important."

"You know the staff talks. We like that you're much different than our last manager," the worker said.

"Yeah, well, that was my goal."

Dane heard the hurt in her voice. He knew every moment she spent working here had to be absolutely soul crushing now that she knew the place would never be hers. She was a damn good manager and had compassion for her staff. She truly cared about this place, these employees.

Stella had just been dismissed in the most uncaring of ways only hours ago. But this morning, she went on with the business-as-usual attitude. She had her pride, sure, but she did this because she didn't want the staff or guests to suffer.

How could he just take everything from her? How could he not want her to be part of this once he took over?

But she wanted the resort to be hers and he simply couldn't allow that to happen. Mirage belonged to him.

Damn that guilt. Not only did the guilt threaten to choke hold him, he didn't know what he'd do once he got home and she wasn't there. She'd been the only person in his entire life to know what he fully suffered from. He'd never let anyone in like he had with Stella. She'd been so easy to talk to, so...

He couldn't find the words. She was everything he didn't know he needed. There was something so therapeutic about her, in the way she genuinely cared, in the way she made everyone else feel like they were the top priority in her life.

But when had anyone made her a priority?

Dane clenched his jaw and shoved the door open to the hallway. He needed to get out and get back to his ranch. An evening with his dogs, his horses, and a ride out in the country would help him think more clearly.

There had to be a way to not ruin Stella's life and still keep everything he'd worked so damn hard for. He just needed to find it.

Dane left the resort, left the mountain, and didn't look back in his rearview mirror. He'd learned the hard way that looking back only kept you in the past. Dane knew only one way to go and that was forward.

From this second on, he'd take charge of Mirage, work with Ethan to destroy Robert and find out some way to make things right for Stella.

Sixteen

After three days of riding horses, drinking bourbon on his enclosed back porch with his dogs at night and messaging back and forth with Ethan, Dane still wasn't calm.

His nerves were on edge. He still hadn't come up with a way to make things right with Stella. He had heard from her—she'd texted him, but he'd replied that he'd have to talk later.

Still taking the coward's way out.

He wanted to offer her the manager position, but deep in his gut he knew she'd turn it down and likely tell him exactly where to take his offer once she realized he was the new owner.

But Stella was exactly the type of person who should be running the resort. Dane was in no position to be hands-on every day—not if he wanted to keep his ranch. Moving permanently to the resort was something he'd have to ease into, even though ultimately that was his goal.

Dane relaxed forward in the front porch swing and rested his elbows on his knees. Buck lay at his feet all curled up, but Bronco sat obediently on the other side waiting on affection.

As he rubbed the soft fur between his dog's ears, Dane ran over and over through his mind what he would say to Stella when he saw her again. There would be no avoiding her, and he didn't want to, but he needed space to sort things out. Even before he left the resort a few days ago, he'd known he needed Stella in the business.

And as much as he wanted to keep thinking of her in that capacity, Dane knew that trail of thoughts barely scratched the surface of everything he remembered when Stella came to mind.

Oh, hell. Who was he kidding? The woman never left his mind. Everything about her clung to his skin even as he dealt with every aspect of daily life. When he'd come home, he'd imagined her here. She'd said more than once that she wanted to escape to the middle of nowhere and unwind. His ranch certainly fit that criteria and now that he was back, he realized just how much he wanted to show her his place.

As the sun set behind the mountain peaks, Dane was glad he was alone. He wasn't in the mood to talk or handle any issues. He just wanted the simplicity of swaying on the swing on his climate-controlled wraparound porch and petting his dogs. His mind was too full of worry and possibilities to consider adding anything else to the mix.

The past few nights since coming home he'd been so damn restless. Sleep hadn't been his friend since returning from the war, but now the dynamics were completely different. He wasn't afraid to go to sleep, he was afraid to wake up without Stella by his side.

When the hell had his heart gotten involved in this charade? That had never been part of his grand plan.

Knowing Stella, as soon as she found out the truth, she'd verbally attack him and make him feel like he wasn't even worthy of being in the same vicinity as her. She had every right to annihilate him, and she would as soon as she learned he was Mirage's new owner. He needed to tell her before she found out some other way.

He needed to be clear where he stood, as the owner, and that he wanted her to remain on board as the manager. Compensating her with a raise and a bonus might go a long way in securing her staying at Mirage. He had to find a way to convince her.

Dane's cell vibrated in his pocket. When he went to grab it, Bronco jerked his head back, giving a glare from the instant lack of attention.

"Hang on, boy."

The alert on his phone was from the gate announcing a visitor. From the video image, he knew who that unexpected guest was and there was no hiding from her anymore.

Dane typed in the code to access the gate and watched as Stella drove her SUV onto his ranch. The drive from the gate to the main house was just over a minute. Not nearly enough time to fine-tune the speech he'd rehearsed because the second she drove through the iron arch with his ranch name, she would know the truth.

A gut-sinking feeling rendered him motionless. His eyes stared off down the driveway, knowing any second he'd see headlights cut through the dusky night.

As dark gray clouds shadowed the sunset, Dane knew another storm was brewing…from all aspects of his life right now.

Dane came to his feet and snapped his fingers, immediately getting his dogs' attention. He opened the front door and put them inside just as those lights cut across his porch.

The knot in his gut tightened, but he remained on the edge of his porch and waited for her to get out of the car. She'd come here for a reason, and had he not deceived her and lied to her face, stealing everything she'd worked for, he might believe that she had come to him to see if there was a chance for them.

Dane wasn't that naive or stupid to think that anything good could come from a fling and a trail of deception. But now that she was here, he had to keep things businesslike and make her understand where he came from. It was time to put all his cards on the table and explain his past with Mirage. Surely she would understand the importance of family, considering that's all she'd wanted for herself.

Sliding his hands into the pockets of his jeans, Dane stared out at the drive as Stella killed the engine. He couldn't see into the windshield that well, but he knew when he looked into her dark eyes, he'd see...

Hell, maybe he didn't know what he'd see. Pain? Regrets? Rage? Likely all of the above.

She didn't get out immediately. Keeping him waiting and wondering was the least that he deserved.

Unable to wait a second longer, Dane made his way down the wide stone steps. The first fat snowflake hit his cheek. His boots scuffed against the concrete drive, but he kept his eyes on that door, waiting.

When he reached the side of her SUV, Dane peered in to see Stella with her head in her hands, her shoulders shaking. Dane jerked on the handle and opened the door. More flakes fell, but he ignored the chill.

"Stella."

Dane started to reach in, but she jerked her head up and slinked back.

"Don't touch me," she commanded as she held him with a watery gaze. "You're nothing but a liar and I'm a damn fool for even coming here."

He didn't know that someone could look so broken, yet so angry at the same time. But Stella was definitely both.

"I *am* a liar, but you're not a fool," he corrected.

Ignoring her plea to leave her alone, Dane reached for her arm and urged her from the vehicle.

"Don't," she cried, tears streaming down her cheeks. "Don't try to make this better. You can't."

No, he couldn't. Stella had taken hit after hit, but this was the first time he'd seen her so broken and completely vulnerable. He'd done this. He'd crushed her more than her father had…which was truly saying something.

The air seemed to turn colder, icier.

"Come inside," he told her. "You can hate me and cry and anything else you want, but we need to get out of this weather."

"I'd rather drive back to Gold Valley through a snowstorm than to be here with you." She pulled her arm away and took a step back. "To think I came here because…"

Dane's heart clenched. There was no way to keep his heart out of this because likely it had been involved from the beginning. Stella drove all this way for him—well, she drove for the man she thought he was.

"You're the new owner," she muttered, then let out a mock laugh. "My father is one hell of an actor because he pretended not to know you."

"He *doesn't* know me," Dane confirmed. "The sale went through my broker and was done in the name of the ranch."

"I'm aware of the ranch name," she scoffed.

The snow came down so thick and fast, the entire area seemed to be blinding white. Dane didn't wait to hear what else she had to say and he didn't ask for permission. She already thought he was a bastard. Might as well go whole hog.

He scooped her up and ran toward the porch. She smacked at his back and cursed him the entire way. Damn she was sexy fired up like this. Not that he'd ever be worthy of having her again. Those memories of their time together were all he'd ever have.

Once he set her down on the porch, Dane kept his hands on her shoulders. He didn't want to force her to do anything, but he didn't want her to bolt before she could hear him out—especially if bolting meant trying to drive in blizzard-like conditions when she was crying and upset. That just sounded like a disaster in the making.

"Why?" she demanded as she stared up at him. She didn't bother swiping at her tears, likely so he'd see the full impact his actions had on her. "Why did you lie to me? Sleeping with me was, what? Just a way to pass the time until you stole my future?"

"No," he defended with a shake of his head. "I... Damn it."

Dane dropped his hands, unable to ignore the agony on her face.

"You came to Mirage purposely to find me," she accused. "Did you laugh when you got me into bed so quickly? I must've made this all so easy on you."

When the wind kicked up and trees cracked outside the window, his dogs started barking their fool heads off. Stella jumped and glanced toward the front door.

"They're not scared," he explained. "When it thunders or gets too windy, they think someone is knocking."

"I can't imagine you get many visitors out here in the middle of nowhere."

He didn't, but his staff would always knock before entering. "Let's get inside," he told her. "You can yell at me all you want there, but I need to get in there before my boys tear up my front door."

"I should leave," she muttered, barely audible over the wind. "I came here thinking we'd see where things went. Now, I want to be anywhere else."

"I get that," he replied. "But it's nasty out there and it's a long drive back to Gold Valley. Might as well stay at least a little longer."

He turned and reached for the door, ready to hold back his dogs so they wouldn't lick Stella to death.

"I don't want to stay," she repeated, but the fight

had left her tone and Dane knew she wasn't going anywhere yet.

She'd never admit her vulnerability, and he admired her for that, but he also knew if he was ever going to get through to her to fully understand his side, then now was the time to explain himself. And Stella deserved an explanation.

Dane stepped over the threshold and gripped his dogs' collars as he hustled them back from the door. Two overly excited golden retrievers wasn't something Stella needed to put up with right now.

Once she was inside and had closed the door, Dane let go of the dogs and snapped his fingers. The boys immediately sat at his side.

"You don't have to stay long, but I need you to hear me out." He stared back at her, knowing she could bolt out of that door at any time, knowing he deserved exactly that. "It's not safe to try to drive right now. You know how Montana weather can be."

Stella's eyes darted down to the dogs and back up to him. "You're used to everyone doing exactly what you want, aren't you?" she sneered. "I'm not going to be that person."

Yet here she was, standing in his foyer.

"Mirage was always meant to be mine," he explained, needing to get to the heart of the issue. "My brother and I both have resorts that were stolen from us before we were old enough or had any power to stop it."

Stella narrowed her eyes. "Stolen? That doesn't even make sense."

Dane ran a hand over his jaw, the stubble raked against his palm. "My mother was Lara Anderson. She built Mirage in Gold Valley and Sunset Cove."

Stella's eyes widened. "That's why you were so determined? Because you think this is owed to you?"

"It is owed to me," he demanded. "Robert Anderson was a complete bastard who took advantage of my mother by marrying her when she was vulnerable after her father's death. When she passed, Ethan and I were still in high school and Robert underhandedly gained rights to those properties and left with our money."

Stella stared at him for a minute before shaking her head and pressing her hand to her eyes. "I can't grasp all of this," she muttered. "I can't figure out how any of this is my fault and why I'm being punished when all I wanted was to have a place of my own, to stand on my own."

Dane took a step forward. "I can help you. I just can't give you Mirage."

Taking a step away from him, Stella leveled his gaze. "I don't want your help. I don't want pity and I don't want…"

Her voice cracked as she trailed off and ultimately turned her back. Dane fisted his hands at his sides, knowing she wanted nothing at all from him at this point. The only thing she'd ever wanted had been ripped from her life…just like it had been ripped from his.

They both wanted Mirage. They both had had the resort pulled away from them when they were so close to obtaining it.

"I know how you feel," he stated. "I've been there. I didn't want to hurt you. I never wanted any of this to harm you in any way. I just wanted what belonged to me."

Stella spun around, her eyes full of fury and unshed tears. "Didn't want me hurt? What did you think would happen? Did you think I'd be so totally blown away by your seduction skills that I'd overlook you jerking my life from me?"

"I never thought that." Though the way she worded it made him sound like an even bigger bastard than he already felt. "I just wanted to find a way to get the resort back in my family like my mother always planned."

"You didn't have to lie to me," she threw back.

Dane gritted his teeth as he tried to find words to defend himself. But she was right. Now that he looked back, now that he realized the impact he'd had on her and how much she'd already been through with her father, she was absolutely right.

The wind kicked up so much the windows rattled. Stella jumped and the dogs started barking again.

Dane snapped his fingers and turned to the dogs. "Bed."

The one-word command had them darting toward the wide stairs and they raced each other up to the second floor. Once they were out of sight, Dane turned back to Stella.

"Come into the living room."

She crossed her arms over her chest. "I'm not staying or obeying your commands."

"You're being ridiculous right now," he growled. "Are you just going to stand in my foyer all night?"

"If I want."

Dane raked a hand over his hair and blew out a sigh. "Don't be so damn stubborn."

Stella stared at him for another minute before she turned her attention around the open space and ultimately went in the opposite direction of the living room.

He glanced up to the ceiling and willed himself to remain calm. This woman had been through hell, at the hands of her father and then him. She was strong willed and angry, and totally entitled to all her frustration and rage.

Having her here at his ranch seemed perfect in all the wrong ways. So as she set off, Dane had no choice but to follow.

Seventeen

Stella figured the storm inside was better to deal with than the storm outside…or at least that's what she told herself as she explored the first level of Dane's ranch.

She wasn't actually focusing on anything, more just wandering aimlessly through the oversize rooms. One area seemed to flow to the next and everything looked like something from a magazine. The high beams, the worn wooden floors, the plush leather sofas, and stone fireplace.

Everything about this house reminded her of the resort. The dark wood, the way everything from the furniture to the size of the rooms just screamed power and money. His mother might have built Mirage, but Dane was clearly his mother's son. Stella was not only fighting her father, but she was also up against a family lineage. Dane wasn't just going to let her have the resort, and she wouldn't expect him to if what he told her was true.

Still, that didn't mean he had gone about things the right way. She wasn't sure what the right way would have been, but she sure as hell knew he'd made the wrong choice.

"Looking for another escape route?" Dane asked as he came up behind her.

Stella turned her attention from the photos lining the mantel to Dane. He stood behind her, just close enough she could reach out and touch him, but far enough to give her a bit of space.

"I'm trying to wrap my head around all of this," she replied honestly. "I mean, what the hell were you thinking coming into all of this? That you deserved Mirage, that you'd get it no matter what and that anything that wasn't your feelings or your end goal simply doesn't matter? Did I sum it all up?"

The muscle clenched in his jaw as he shoved his hands into his pockets. Those dark eyes narrowed.

"Don't even try to be offended," she went on. "You brought all of this upon yourself."

"I had no time," he demanded. "It's not just Mirage in Gold Valley. There's more going on and I had to move when I could."

"More what? More businesses you're trying to steal from unsuspecting women?"

He stared at her for another minute before cursing under his breath and turning to pace toward the wall of windows. The harsh conditions continued to rage outside and honestly, it wasn't much prettier inside. She wished she'd never come. She wished she'd never met Dane Michaels. And she wished like hell she'd never put stock in thinking her father would finally give her something—anything—she truly wanted.

She'd felt so damn isolated for so long. Even training for the competitions she'd felt alone because not many people understood that willpower and determination.

Now here she was alone. Stella knew she needed to dig deep and find that drive and determination all over again. She would, too. Nothing would keep her down. Life may knock her, but she couldn't let the hits deter her.

Stella stared at Dane across the room. He'd not answered her and from his rigid shoulders and silence, she had a feeling he wasn't planning on it, either.

She turned back to the photos on the mantel. There were only three. There were two on each end and each picture was a teenage version of Dane with another boy who she assumed was his brother, and their mother. The photo in the middle of the mantel was a snapshot of his mother alone. Her head was thrown back as she laughed and there was so much happiness, so much life in that image.

Tears formed once again and Stella wished she didn't feel for this woman, this man. But Lara Anderson was the woman Stella had admired for years. Stella had loved hearing the story about Lara and how she'd started the resorts for couples…yet she was a single mother with two boys.

There was a family here in these photos, a family Stella had always wanted and craved. But this family had been torn apart by an untimely death and Dane just wanted to reclaim what he believed belonged to him.

She turned back to find him staring directly at her. Her stomach tightened. That darkened stare had her nerves on edge. She didn't want to see this side of him. She didn't want to see him as a human with real feelings. From the second she turned into the drive and saw that iron arch with the ranch name, Dane had become a complete stranger. She didn't know where the man was from the resort, but damn if her heart didn't have a hole in it that was just his size.

She could walk away, no matter how much it hurt, if she could convince herself that everything about that man she'd thought he was had been a lie. But the longer she stayed, the more she realized the truth was complicated—and so was Dane.

"I realize we're not that different," she stated. "We both want the same thing for justifiable reasons."

Dane started forward, but Stella held up her hands and kept going. "Your methods are clearly what sets us apart. I never would've used someone, blindsided them, and then stolen their life."

"You really think your dad was just going to turn the resort over to you?"

Stella's heart clenched. "Maybe not, but I had a fighting chance before you came along throwing your money and whatever else at him."

Dane crossed his arms over his chest and clenched his jaw. "I gave him two of my businesses on top of the money."

Part of her admired the lengths he would go to in order to reclaim his mother's legacy. The other part of her, the part that had been manipulated, hated every part of Dane Michaels for going behind her back to steal what she'd thought could be hers.

But damn if she wasn't still attracted to him. Her body still responded to that midnight gaze, those broad shoulders…one glimpse of those talented hands.

Why couldn't there be some switch to turn off emotions and tingly reactions? Sex messed with her head. Great sex somehow managed to mess with her heart because there was no way she'd fallen for him. Stella refused to believe that she could have in such a short time.

"You're thinking."

Dane's words settled between them. That low tone

always got to her in ways she'd never been able to explain. How could a voice cause arousal?

But, yes, she was thinking. Thinking how she was stuck here waiting for the storm to pass. Thinking about how she'd been used. Thinking about how the past few weeks had been out of her control and she wanted to take that control back.

Stella took a step toward Dane before she could talk herself out of this. If she thought too much she'd find every reason not to take this leap. But for now, just for this moment, she was in charge and she'd be damned if anyone else would ever take the decisions from her again.

"I hate you," she told him as she started working on the buttons on her dress. "I hate how you stole my world from me. But you're right. You are the same man who stayed in my bed when I was exhausted and alone, who helped me when I didn't even ask. You're the same man my body craves and the man I can't stop wanting."

"Stella—"

"No." She shrugged out of her dress, sending it to the floor in a whisper. "I call the shots now. You used me, right? Well, I'm about to use you. I want you and I'm going to have you."

Dane's eyes widened, his jaw clenched and his nostrils flared. She recognized his signs of arousal and desire. His gaze raked over her nearly bare body.

She had on only her knee boots and her matching nude lace bra and panties.

"This isn't a good idea," he told her. "You know it's not. Are you doing this to get back at me?"

Stella shrugged. "Perhaps. But I'm also doing it because I want you. I wish I could turn that off, but I see you and my body responds."

She quickly rid herself of her boots before focusing on him again. "Unless you've decided you've gotten all you wanted from me."

Dane muttered a curse before he was on her. "I should turn you away, but damn if you don't have some power over me."

He scooped her up and started back toward the entryway, back toward the steps.

"Not your bedroom," she commanded.

There was no way she'd go somewhere that personal, that intimate.

"This isn't anything more than sex," she added.

Dane set her back on her feet and backed her against the wide door frame leading from the living room. For a half second, he merely stared, seeming to take in her entire body with one hungry sweep.

Then he thrust his hands through her hair and captured her lips. Stella arched her body and found the edge of his T-shirt. With frantic motions, she jerked it up, pulling her lips away long enough to get the shirt up and over his head. Then he was on her again as she went for his belt and the snap on his jeans.

She'd barely gotten them unzipped when he pulled away. Dane kept his eyes on her while he reached into his pocket and pulled out protection. He covered himself and stepped back toward her.

Stella opened for him, threading her fingers through his hair, and taking everything he gave. Part of her knew this was wrong, but the devil on her shoulder thought it was a great idea. There was nothing wrong with taking charge and allowing pleasure. There was nothing wrong with going into this moment with her eyes wide-open and her heart shut tight.

When Dane gripped her waist and lifted her, Stella's thoughts vanished. All she knew was passion as she wrapped her legs around his waist and sank onto him. Clutching his shoulders, she closed her eyes and pressed her back against the solid door frame. Dane's lips trailed over the column of her neck, over her sensitive breasts. He palmed her backside as he pumped his hips and Stella just let the euphoric sensations wash over her.

Dane muttered something as he traveled back up to the erogenous area just below her ear.

That was all it took for her body to respond and spiral out of control. All of her emotions balled up together and she gave herself over to the climax. This was why she'd decided to surprise him. She'd needed to be with him, needed to feel him.

Stella's entire body shook and all thoughts vanished. She kept her eyes shut, needing to keep her emotions locked inside and not look too closely at him. She just wanted to feel.

Dane murmured something in her ear, she only made out the word "need" but she ignored it as he jerked his hips harder. His body tightened, his fingertips dug into her backside, and Stella dropped her head to his shoulder as he took his own pleasure.

His heated body stuck to hers, and Stella didn't want to lift her head. She didn't want to face reality.

But she knew this was it. She and Dane were done...if they'd ever really started. They'd had a fling, that was all. Though she'd thought there was more, there couldn't be. He'd deceived her, slept with her under false pretenses and then left without a word. At any time he could've given her the truth, but he'd chosen to keep his true self hidden away.

The same way she'd have to hide away the fact she'd fallen in love with the man she thought he was.

Pulling together all of her strength and resolve, Stella extracted herself from the warmth and strength she'd only experienced from Dane. She hated him for making her hate him. That sounded so messed up in her own thoughts, but he'd damaged something inside her. Something she didn't know if she'd recover from.

He didn't say a word as he stepped from the room. Stella dressed in a hurry, not caring if her buttons were straight or her hair was in knots. She had to go. Staying here, waiting on him to state another defense, would only make her thoughts, her heart, even more muddled.

Just as she zipped up her boot and came to her feet, Dane stepped back into the room.

"You want to talk about this?" he asked.

"Nothing to discuss." Did that even sound convincing? "You used me, I used you."

"Is that what this was?" he asked, crossing his arms over his chest and leaning against the very spot he'd just taken her. "You wanted to retaliate? Doesn't seem like you."

Stella swallowed and tipped her chin. "Seems we didn't know each other as well as we thought."

She crossed to the doorway, easily moving past him in the large opening.

"Where are you going?"

Tossing a look over her shoulder, she replied, "The storm has passed."

"What about us?"

Gripping the doorknob, Stella turned away and whispered, "That's passed, too."

Eighteen

Mirage wasn't near as inviting as it had been.

For the past month, he'd been back and forth between the resort and the ranch. More at the resort, though, since he needed to acclimate the staff to his management style and get up-to-date with the various systems.

Ethan had told Dane to hold off on coming because something had held Robert up and it looked like he wasn't going to be coming for a bit. Dane certainly had things he could be doing here to bide his time.

His first order had been to fire the asshole who'd disrespected Stella. Apparently he'd also been the spy, hence the cockiness since he worked directly with Ruiz.

Dane's second order had been to get his attorney and accountant on-site to see what the hell he could do to get Stella back here—where she belonged.

That had been over three weeks ago and he'd still not heard a word from her. He'd known full well she'd received the employment offer and he didn't know what was taking her so damn long to respond. Though her silence was nothing less than he deserved.

Damn it. Nobody just flat-out ignored him. Never. Not even when he had it coming. He might be a recluse, he might shy away from getting too involved with crowds of people, but that didn't mean he was soft or ready to just give up.

Dane knew he had to give Stella time. Her entire world had been shattered and he'd precipitated it all. Now he was trying to piece all those shards back together and without seeing her, he had no idea if his tactics were even working.

Since she'd walked out of his house after using him, he'd been destroyed. He didn't care that she'd wanted to use his body. Their physical connection couldn't be just ignored or brushed aside. There was no way someone as caring and loving as Stella could just walk away and not think or feel anymore.

And there was love looking back at him when she'd been in his home. He'd seen it, felt it.

And he knew he'd fallen just as hard.

Dane turned the corner heading to his office at

Mirage. He nearly ran into one of the receptionists, but quickly put his hands out to stop her from plowing into him.

"Oh, Mr. Michaels," she gasped. "I'm so sorry."

Dane might still be struggling with some names of his new employees, but not Lola. He remembered her quite well.

"I've told you to call me Dane," he reminded her, as he'd done every single day he'd been there. "You worked for my mother."

Lola smiled and smoothed her cropped, gray hair from her forehead. "That may be, and I may remember you as a thirteen-year-old boy, but that doesn't mean anything now. You're my boss and I respect that."

"I appreciate the respect, but Dane will be just fine," he confirmed. "You've been here since the beginning. I hope you'll stay on."

Lola nodded and patted his arm. "I wouldn't dream of leaving. Your mother would be so proud of you."

Guilt threatened to choke him, but so did a rush of warmth at the kind comment. Story of his life lately. He'd destroyed one woman he loved while honoring the other.

"Oh, Stella is in your office," Lola added.

Dane jerked. "Excuse me?"

"Stella Garcia," Lola repeated. "She said she had an appointment, so I let her in. I was getting ready to call you. I hope that was okay."

The worry in her tone had Dane offering a smile. "That was more than okay. Thanks, Lola."

He skirted around the faithful employee in an effort to get to his office. Dane didn't care that he looked like a madman racing down the hall. There was only so much control a guy could have and he'd waited long enough for Stella to get back with him about his offer.

Granted, he'd thought she'd call, but an in-person meeting was sure as hell something he wasn't about to turn down.

Dane opened the door to his office and stepped inside to find Stella in his new leather office chair behind his desk.

She glanced from his computer screen to him as she propped those long bare legs up on the corner of his desk.

Just the sight of her had his gut tightening, his heart pumping faster. He leaned against the door and closed it with his back. She didn't have on boots today like she typically did with her dresses. No, today she had on heels meant for the bedroom and a little red suit that looked like it was made of wrapping paper it was so damn tight…in all the right places.

If he needed to hire someone to torture guests, she'd be the woman for the job. She was killing him.

"Your minion gave me the message," she stated. "Was that some type of a joke?"

Dane hooked his thumbs through his belt loops

and shook his head. "Not a joke at all. I just didn't confront you myself because I knew you needed time."

"Time?" Those legs slid off his desk with grace and Stella came to her feet. She smoothed her skirt down to mid-thigh and circled the desk. "You proposed marriage through a damn letter that my attorney delivered from your attorney."

Dane swallowed. "I guess the proposal could use some work, but I figured if I asked in person you'd punch me—and then you'd say no. I can take a punch, but I didn't want you to turn me down."

Stella stared across the room. With her brows drawn in, her hands on her hips, her jacket pulling across pert breasts...she was damn breathtaking.

"Turn you down?" she repeated. "Of course I'm turning you down. You're insane. I'm not marrying you."

"Did you read the entire letter?"

"The part where I'd be part owner of Mirage? Yes." She licked her lips, probably not knowing how arousing that was. Now was certainly not the time to bring it up. "I don't know where this came from, but I'm not marrying you. If you feel guilty for taking all of this from me, that's on you. You can't just ask someone to marry you because your feelings are all out of whack."

Dane took a step toward her, then another, until they stood toe-to-toe. "You could've ripped up the letter and ignored me," he told her, reaching to brush a strand of hair from her cheek. He let his fingertips feather across her jaw as he continued. "You could've texted or even called. Yet here you are."

"I needed to—"

"See me?" he asked, sliding his other hand up to frame her face. "Damn, I've missed you."

Stella closed her eyes. "Don't say that. We are nothing, Dane."

He remained silent, waiting for her to finish the silent war no doubt waging in her head. After a moment, her lids fluttered and she focused on him.

"You don't want to marry me, you want to sleep with me," she told him.

Dane couldn't suppress the smile. "Why can't I do both?"

On a groan, Stella backed away and shook her head. "Because this is reality and the reality is I can't be with someone who lied to and deceived me."

Dane pulled in a shaky breath. He deserved that, but the words still hurt. He reminded himself that she was here, in his office, so not all hope was lost.

"You came to my house and slept with me," he started. "I know you claimed you were using me and it was just physical, but that's not the Stella I know. You love me."

Her eyes widened, her mouth opened, but nothing came out. She quickly snapped her lips shut and set her jaw.

"Even after you realized who I was," he went on, "you still wanted me. That's not ego, that's facts."

Stella shrugged. "So what? Yes, I fell in love with you, but that's not real. I fell in love with the person I thought you were. I don't even know the real you."

"You know me more than anyone else in my life. I've told you things, opened up about my past. I wouldn't do that with someone I didn't care about or someone I was just casually sleeping with."

When she didn't snap back with an answer, Dane hoped there was some part of her that believed him. He couldn't stop this momentum now.

"I fully admit I sought you out as part of my strategy to retake ownership of this place," Dane admitted. "I didn't set out to purposely hurt you and once I got to know you…"

"What?" she demanded. "You magically grew a soul?"

Dane couldn't hide his emotions and quickly realized Stella didn't want him to. She deserved to know exactly how he felt, his every thought on this matter.

"Once I got to know you, I realized deceiving you wasn't how my mom would want me to go about getting the resort back," he explained.

Unable to stand still or to look at that hurt in Stella's dark eyes, Dane started walking around the spacious office. He went to the wall of windows that overlooked the snowy mountain peaks.

"My mom wanted this place to be mine. There was no doubt about that. When I lost it, I knew that one day when I had the money and the power, I'd get it all back. This has been my goal since I was eighteen."

Dane turned back around and leaned against the cool glass. "Now that it's mine, I'm not near as happy as I thought I'd be. Everything is empty without you—the resort, my life. My heart."

Unshed tears swam in her eyes and he couldn't keep this distance between them another second. Dane crossed to her and took her by the shoulders.

"If you believe nothing else, you have to believe that I love you."

Stella reached up and swiped at his cheek and Dane realized he'd let his emotions show a little too well. He hadn't even noticed the tear. His only concern had been getting her to see that he hadn't lied about everything.

"I'll give the entire place to you," he told her. "If you still want it, it's yours."

Stella gasped and jerked back. "What?"

Dane's hands dropped to his sides. He couldn't believe after all of these years, all of this work, he was saying this, but he meant it.

"My mother was proud of this place, she had a goal of passing it to me." Dane raked a hand over the back of his neck and sighed. "But she wouldn't want me ruining lives in order to reclaim it."

"Dane."

"She would've loved you," he murmured, the damn emotions threatening to strangle him. "She would've loved you not only because I love you, but because you're a kick-ass businesswoman."

Stella laughed and closed the distance between them. Those tears swimming in her eyes threatened to spill at any moment.

"Say it again," she demanded.

"I love you, Stella." He smoothed her hair from her face, sliding his thumb along her bottom lip. "I thought I did before you found out who I was, but I was too afraid to admit it—I knew you'd eventually learn the truth and that it would ruin everything between us, so I tried to convince myself it wouldn't wreck me to lose you. I want you to have this place. You may not be ready for marriage, but you deserve this."

Stella fisted his hair and pulled his mouth to hers. Dane didn't miss a chance to wrap his arms around her and pull her in. It had been too damn long.

When she broke the kiss and leaned back, her eyes shone bright with tears and her smile filled those cracks in his heart.

"I want the resort, but I want you, too," she told him. "Do you think your mother would be on board with both of us running this? I'm not sure that marriage is our next step. We probably should slow down a bit so we don't mess this up again, but that doesn't mean we have to be apart."

"I'll go as slow as you want," he told her, smacking her lips with his. "And I'm the one who messed up before. But I sure as hell won't take you for granted ever again. We're equals, Stella. In business and in life."

"Can I make a confession?" she asked.

"What's that?"

"I don't have anything on under my suit."

Dane's body instantly responded. "Miss Garcia, is this how you plan to conduct all of our business meetings?"

She stepped from his arms and went to the door. With a flick of her wrist, the dead bolt clicked into place. Stella turned back around and started working on the buttons of her jacket.

"I hope that won't be a problem," she asked. "I didn't think my new business partner would mind."

Dane closed the distance between them and finished unwrapping his woman. "Oh, he definitely doesn't mind."

As he pulled her into his arms, he realized that the emptiness in his life that he'd felt ever since losing his mother had healed at last. Here in this place, with this woman beside him, he knew he was exactly where he belonged.

He was finally home.

* * * * *

Don't miss Ethan's story!
California Secrets
Available September 2019!

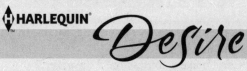
#2683 TEXAS-SIZED SCANDAL
Texas Cattleman's Club: Houston • by Katherine Garbera
Houston philanthropist Melinda Perry always played by the rules. Getting pregnant by a mob boss's son was certainly never in the playbook—until now. Can they contain the fallout...and maybe even turn their forbidden affair into forever?

#2684 STRANDED AND SEDUCED
Boone Brothers of Texas • by Charlene Sands
To keep her distance from ex-fling Risk Boone, April Adams pretends to be engaged. But when a storm strands them together and the rich rancher has an accident resulting in amnesia, he suddenly thinks he's the fiancé! Especially when passion overtakes them...

#2685 BLACK TIE BILLIONAIRE
Blackout Billionaires • by Naima Simone
CEO Gideon Knight demands that Shay Neal be his fake fiancée to avenge his family. Too bad he doesn't realize they already shared an anonymous night during the Chicago blackout! But even through the deception, the truth of their chemistry cannot be denied.

#2686 CALIFORNIA SECRETS
Two Brothers • by Jules Bennett
Ethan Michaels is on a mission to reclaim the resort his mother built. Then he's sidetracked by sexy Harper Williams—only to find out she's his enemy's daughter. All's fair in love and war...until Harper's next explosive secret shakes Ethan to his core.

#2687 A BET WITH BENEFITS
The Eden Empire • by Karen Booth
Entrepreneur Mindy Eden scoffs when her sisters bet she can't spend time with her real estate mogul ex without succumbing to temptation. But it soon becomes crystal clear that second chances are in the cards. Will Mindy risk her business for one more shot at pleasure?

#2688 POWER PLAY
The Serenghetti Brothers • by Anna DePalo
Hockey legend and sports industry tycoon Jordan Serenghetti needs his injury healed—and fast. Too bad he clashes with his physical therapist over a kiss they once shared—and Jordan forgot! As passions flare, will she be ready for more revelations from his player past?

SPECIAL EXCERPT FROM

HQN™

For Vanessa Logan, returning home was about healing,
not exploring her attraction to cowboy Jacob Dalton!
But walking away from their explosive chemistry is
proving impossible…

Read on for a sneak preview of
Lone Wolf Cowboy *by* New York Times *and*
USA TODAY *bestselling author Maisey Yates.*

She curled her hands into fists, grabbing hold of his T-shirt.
And she had no idea what the hell was running through her
head as she stood there looking up into those wildly blue
eyes, the present moment mingling with memories of that
night long ago.

While he witnessed the deepest, darkest thing she'd ever
gone through. Something no one else even knew about.

He was the only one who knew.

The only one who knew what had started everything.
Olivia didn't understand. Her parents didn't understand.
And they had never wanted to understand.

But he knew. He knew and he had already seen what a
disaster she was.

There was no facade to protect. No new enlightened
sense of who she was. No narrative about her as a lost cause
out there roaming the world.

He'd already seen her break apart. For real. Not the
Vanessa that existed when she was hiding. Hiding her
problems from her family. Hiding her feelings behind a high.

Hiding. And more hiding.

No. He had seen her at her lowest when she hadn't been able to hide.

And somehow, he seemed to bring that out in her. Because she wasn't able to hide her anger.

And she wasn't able to hide this. Whatever the wildness was that was coursing through her veins. No, she couldn't hide that either. And she wasn't sure she cared.

So she was just going to let the wildness carry her forward.

She couldn't remember the last time she had done that. The last time she'd allowed herself this pure kind of over-the-top emotion.

It had been pain. The pain she felt that night she lost the baby. That was the last time she had let it all go. In all the time since then when she had been on the verge of being overwhelmed by emotion she had crushed it completely. Hidden it beneath drugs. Hidden it beneath therapy speak.

She had carefully kept herself in hand since she'd gotten sober. Kept herself under control.

What she hadn't allowed herself to do was feel.

She was feeling now. And she wasn't going to stop it.

She launched herself forward, and her lips connected with his.

And before she knew it, she was kissing Jacob Dalton with all the passion she hadn't known existed inside of her.

Don't miss
Lone Wolf Cowboy *by Maisey Yates,*
available August 2019 wherever
Harlequin® *books and ebooks are sold.*

www.Harlequin.com

PHMYEXP0819

CEO Gideon Knight demands that Shay Neal be his fake fiancée to avenge his family. Too bad he doesn't realize they already shared an anonymous night during the Chicago blackout! But even through the deception, the truth of their chemistry cannot be denied.

Read on for a sneak peek at
Black Tie Billionaire
by USA TODAY *bestselling author Naima Simone!*

"To answer your other question," he murmured. "Why did I single you out? Your first guess was correct. Because you are so beautiful I couldn't help following you around this over-the-top ballroom filled with people who possess more money than sense. The women here can't outshine you. They're like peacocks, spreading their plumage, desperate to be noticed, and here you are among them, like the moon. Bright, alone, above it all and eclipsing every one of them. What I don't understand is how no one else noticed before me. Why every man in this place isn't standing behind me in a line just for the chance to be near you."

Silence swelled around them like a bubble, muting the din of the gala. His words seemed to echo in the cocoon, and he marveled at them. Hadn't he sworn he didn't do pretty words? Yet it had been him talking about peacocks and moons.

What was she doing to him?

Even as the question echoed in his mind, her head tilted back and she stared at him, her lovely eyes darker...hotter. In that moment, he'd stand under a damn balcony and serenade her if she continued looking at him like that. He curled his fingers into his palm, reminding himself with the pain that he couldn't touch her. Still, the only sound that reached his ears was the quick, soft pants breaking on her pretty lips.

"I—I need to go," she whispered, already shifting back and away from him. "I—" She didn't finish the thought, but turned and waded into the crowd, distancing herself from him.

He didn't follow; she hadn't said no, but she hadn't said yes, either. And though he'd caught the desire in her gaze— his stomach still ached from the gut punch of it—she had to come to him.

Or ask him to come for her.

Rooted where she'd left him, he tracked her movements.

Saw the moment she cleared the mass of people and strode in the direction of the double doors where more tray-bearing staff emerged and exited.

Saw when she paused, palm pressed to one of the panels.

Saw when she glanced over her shoulder in his direction.

Even across the distance of the ballroom, the electric shock of that look whipped through him, sizzled in his veins. Moments later, she disappeared from view. Didn't matter; his feet were already moving in her direction.

That glance, that look. It'd sealed her fate.

Sealed it for both of them.

What will happen when these two find each other alone during the blackout?

Find out in
Black Tie Billionaire
*by USA TODAY bestselling author Naima Simone
available September 2019 wherever
Harlequin® Desire books and ebooks are sold.*

www.Harlequin.com

  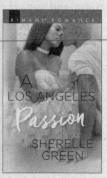